For my crazy mixed up family.
Thank you for believing in my dream.

Wrapped Up in Beau

First Levi Lynn Books edition November 2019.

Levi Lynn Books can bring authors to your live event. For more information or to book an event, visit our website at www.miaheintzelman.com.

Editing by Danielle Acee and Danylle Salinas

Cover design and Formatting by Tangled Covers

Manufactured in the United States of America

Cataloguing-in-Publication Data

Name: Heintzelman, Mia, author.

Title: Wrapped Up in Beau / Mia Heintzelman

Description: Mia Heintzelman | Las Vegas: Mia Heintzelman, 2019.

Subjects: Romance | Humorous fiction | Seasonal

WRAPPED UP IN BEAU

MIA HEINTZELMAN

IT'S BEGINNING TO LOOK A LOT LIKE CHRISTMAS

*B*eau Redgrave stopped typing mid-sentence. An email notification popped up in the corner of his screen, bouncing and cheerful before it fell away, taking his attention with it. It was three weeks into December, and finally it was beginning to feel like Christmas.

A slow smile tugged at the corners of his mouth as his finger hovered over the mouse.

"Redgrave, did you check your email?"

Beau blinked out of his trance and swiveled the chair around to find his best friend Shane propped against the doorframe, his arms folded, and brows waggling like crazy.

"Looks like Christmas came early, huh, bro? Should I get some wrapping paper and one of those obnoxious, giant red bows? I don't know, it might fit under the tree."

Beau rolled his eyes. "Relax. I saw the message pop up, but I haven't read it yet. Besides, why are you even still here? It's Thursday. Shouldn't you be at some casino playing craps or roulette or something?"

Shane ignored him.

"I know you've been in here overthinking shit. Stop," Shane

said. "I'll give you the rundown. McAllister is leaving, which means there's an opening, and you've basically got this shit in the bag." The cheeky asshole that he was, he fist-pumped the air like he was at a football game and he was winning somehow. "Davenport literally asked you, point-blank in front of everyone at the meeting last quarter, if you were interested in the position." His arms dramatically flailed in the air. "He probably knew about this then!"

Hell, I knew about this then.

"As far as I'm concerned, no one else is even remotely qualified to compete with you," Shane added.

Beau started a slow clap. "Are you finished? I haven't even read the message." He turned and toggled to his email with Shane breathing over his shoulder. He clicked the most recent message.

> John McAllister has stepped down from the
> regional wealth management team, effec-
> tive immediately, to pursue other oppor-
> tunities outside the company…

Beau didn't have to finish reading the message to know what happened. This was not a one-off. The guy didn't "step down." He was pushed out, canned right here on the holidays because he couldn't do the long hours and the late nights with a wife and kids waiting for him at home.

The word "couldn't" snagged Beau's thoughts. *Couldn't, or wouldn't?* There was a difference.

Beau, on the other hand, had nothing but time and no one waiting at home.

Anymore.

He wasn't the one who gave up.

It wasn't just this promotion. That was all sorted. He knew all about asking, believing, and receiving. He subscribed to all of the motivational tactics about the secrets to a fulfilled life. He'd read the books about leaping, jumping, and forging ahead in the face of cowardice critics. There wasn't a Netflix video or TED Talk about taking life by the balls he didn't watch. In his mind, there were people who persevered in the face of challenge and those who walked out.

"So…are you going to call Davenport, or what?" Shane asked.

"Yeah," Beau said, absently nodding, but his mind was set. It's what life was about—you keep your head down, work hard, and you get the rewards.

"Heck, yes." Shane grunted. He polished off his coffee and pointed toward Beau with the cup. He was amped. As long as they'd been working together, they always said one of them had to make it to the top. "You look like you need caffeine. I'm going to grab more. Want some?"

"Brilliant."

As soon as Shane left, Beau sighed, and for the first time since he put it there, he dug into the bottom drawer of his desk and pulled out the framed picture of him and Bree. It was the night he proposed…the night she said yes. He was on bended knee and she was crying—happy tears because they had made plans and promises.

A beep sounded on his phone before the receptionist's voice droned through on the intercom. "Line two is for you. I tried to take a message, but she said it's urgent."

"Right, okay. Thanks." He replaced the photo in the drawer and shut it. He pressed the button to connect the line and leaned back in his chair, letting his head fall back. His mind was heavy. "This is Beau Redgrave."

"Good morning. This is Dr. Ryan at Northwestern Memorial Hospital. I'm calling regarding Hattie Redgrave. She's listed you as her next of kin—"

"What happened?" *Fuck.* Beau righted himself in the chair, pressing his fingers to his lips. His heart pounded as he waited, worry gnawing at him. "Is she—?"

The doctor cleared her throat. "She's doing well now, sleeping at the moment, but she's asked to see you."

No.

His blood ran cold as fear clawed at him. He couldn't lose his grandmother, too. For a moment, he was paralyzed, crumbling on the inside. His body felt leaden at the thought of losing the only family he had left. Right now, nothing else seemed to matter. All he could think about was how he'd brushed her off for Thanksgiving and planned to fly in Christmas Eve only to leave the day after the holiday.

He blew out a breath to clear his head. "Are you able to give me any details? She's diabetic."

"Yes. Her blood sugar level is low and she had a hypoglycemic episode. There's no new information at this time, but she has been admitted. We'll be sure to notify you with any updates as they come in."

When he disconnected the line, Beau immediately searched the flights to Chicago from Las Vegas. He'd accumulated a few hundred thousand miles, which were just sitting there since he hardly ever went anywhere. The only flight he could get on out of McCarran tonight was a red-eye with a forty-five minute layover, connecting in Denver.

Later that night, after he'd parked in the long-term lot, checked in, and made his way through the security checkpoint, Beau took the tram over to the terminal. Of course, his gate was the farthest one. He checked his watch. Still ten minutes until boarding.

He slowed his pace and cracked his neck, adjusting his leather duffle on his shoulder. His neck felt tight, and he had a splitting headache from worry. Just thinking about his grandmother lying there in a hospital bed, helpless and weak, was killing him. She was already frail the last time he saw her in May.

Beau wrung his fingers. He should have gone back for Thanksgiving and maybe he might have seen the signs and been able to stop this from happening. He should have been there this time.

A slot machine chimed in the distance as he approached the gate. Quickly, he slipped his ID and ticket out and waited off to the side of the boarding area. It was quiet, but the jingling sound of the song, "It's Beginning to Look a Lot Like Christmas" played beneath the hum of people talking and flight announcements.

He finally took in his surroundings. Lit garland draped from the ceiling, topped off with gigantic, vibrant red bows and flying white doves. There were poinsettias at every corner and wreaths adorned with colorful bulb ornaments. It was all beautiful, but not nearly as the vision right in front of him.

He inhaled a sharp intake of air.

A small wisp of a woman with an hourglass shape and long, glossy auburn waves pulled into a loose ponytail stood in line at the counter with her phone pressed to her ear, deep in conversation. Her posture was ramrod straight and her feet slightly turned out from years of ballet. It was the charm bracelet on her right wrist that gave her away. Beau would know her anywhere, but only in this moment did he realize how much he'd missed seeing her face.

Even with only the angle of her profile, she was stunning. She was casually dressed in jeans with black rainboots and a smart black blazer over a pink blouse and still alarmingly gorgeous.

Beau pressed the pads of his fingers softly to his lips as a breath hitched in his throat.

Bree.

*A*ubrey Green squished the phone between her ear and shoulder while she plucked out her laptop and flipped it open. "Mom, seriously? Can you not? Yes, I have the book you sent me, and you know I'm still not seeing anyone. I'm at the airport now. I'll be there in time for Matt's party."

In her ear, her mother continued to list the many reasons why she needed to be back home in Chicago sooner rather than later. Aside from the fact that Aubrey was being seriously guilt-tripped for not coming home in over six months, there was a boatload of family coming into town expecting to see her. Apparently, her brother's life would come to a screeching halt if she wasn't present when he "surprised" Sabrina by popping the question.

Except, Aubrey knew better. She followed Sabrina on Instagram and it was more than obvious she was in on the big to-do. Her usual purple hair was now a mousy shade of brown. Her skintight clothing was replaced with Jackie O.-style dresses with three-quarter-length sleeves that covered her tattoos.

That was mother/life-curator Ellen Green for you—less Kris Jenner and more Martha Stewart. Aubrey had no doubts whose manicured hands were dabbling in the cookie jar. There was no way in hell her mother would let any daughter of hers—or, daughter-in-law-to-be—step foot out in front of her family and friends without organizing and planning the play-by-play.

The overhead speaker cracked and made a ear-piercing screech.

"At this time, we'll now be boarding our premier-class passengers."

Aubrey flicked a glance up at the plastic-perfect gate agent who made the announcement.

Thank you.

"Um, okay. I need to get going," Aubrey said, knowing good and well it would be at least another ten minutes until they got to her seat. Based on the cheap fare she got by crazy chance, she was surprised she was even on the plane and not underneath with the lavatory release valve.

"Well, all right, honey. Just so you know, I can't tell you the details now, but I have a *special* surprise for you. I *know* you're going to love it. I just pray you have the decency to get here on time. You know how fickle the weather is this time of year. All I need is to have you come straggling in and mess up—"

"They just called my seat. Love you. Bye." The words skidded out fast and sticky, but Aubrey needed to end the call for sanity reasons. She was vaguely interested in the "special surprise," but it didn't seem worth the nagging. She hung up just before her brain short-circuited and caught fire.

Lord, that woman knew how to work her nerve.

She pinched the bridge of her nose for a second and looked up just in time to see him boarding.

What. The. Fuck?

She would know that strong jaw line, amber brown skin, and those piercing gray eyes anywhere. Her pulse quickened and her heart tripped around in her chest. Heat crawled up her neck.

Beau.

On my plane.

God he looks good. Better than good, he looked…breezy and carefree. Like his life was so much better without her in it. He'd always been disarmingly handsome with his tall, athletic build, but his shoulders seemed broader. He probably spent his days in the gym flirting with unmotivated girls who had no dreams other than to be his little wife.

Ugh.

She was completely losing her shit.

"Holy…" She pressed her fist to her lips, afraid to say more.

"Everything okay?" a man in glasses waiting beside her asked. He barely came up to her shoulders and had a serious case of casual CEO fashion sense with a polo tucked and belted into his pleated jeans. He had all of his hair on the sides but was completely bald on top. His eyes were kind, though.

He smiled and she smiled back despite her explosive nerves and heartbeat sounding off in her ears.

She glanced back over to the plane door, but Beau was gone.

She jammed her hands into her coat pockets, found the small hole in the corner, weaseled her finger inside it, and exhaled an anxious breath. "Yeah. I just…thought I saw someone I knew."

"Happens to me all the time," the guy said. "I look up and wave, the person waves back and I smile. I think, *yeah that is Joe Schmoe,* but then I walk over and realize he was waving at someone behind me and I feel like a complete idiot."

With her shitty luck, that wasn't the end of his story. Or, rather stories, plural, it turned out. He'd saved up a whole arsenal of tidbits like that one for the first innocent bystander with a friendly smile.

Aubrey was getting less friendly by the second. She could feel the tight smile and confusion twisting her face.

He's a Chatty Cathy. Please don't let me be sitting next to this guy. Lord, please. If he was, she probably wouldn't have enough time during the flight to work on her article due Monday, not that she could concentrate knowing Beau was on the same plane.

Seriously? He hates red-eyes.

"Okay, well." She looked over her shoulder hopefully. "They should be calling us any minute. Hope you have a good flight."

She pivoted, but realized she couldn't go far. They *were* about to call her seat number.

"That's some collection of charms you've got there," Chatty continued, leaning in for a closer look. In addition to having no verbal filter, it seemed he also had no spatial boundaries.

Aubrey clamped her eyes shut and prayed this whole nightmare would end. It was childish, but maybe this was like playing peek-a-boo with a toddler—if she closed her eyes, neither Chatty nor Beau would see her.

SILENT NIGHT

*B*eau tightened his seatbelt, gripped both armrests, and leaned his head back against the seat, closing his eyes.

"Flight attendants, please prepare for takeoff," the captain announced over the intercom.

A baby somewhere back in coach began to wail as the plane, shaking and rumbling, raced down the tarmac. Above him, he could hear luggage shifting in the overhead bin. He peeked into the aisle, but the cabin was pitch-black.

Then…liftoff.

Thank God, I got the aisle seat.

His bladder was full, and the restroom was only a few steps away.

It had been over six months since he'd flown, but it was never *this* bad. He was on edge. Every nerve ending in his body pulsed and his heart pounded in his ears. Deep down, he knew this had nothing to do with flying and everything to do with the woman sitting two-dozen rows behind him. They were thousands of feet in the air, floating in a confined metal vessel, but still a million miles away from each other.

As soon as the plane leveled off and the flight attendants began moving around the cabin, Beau pulled out his laptop. He should be working or sending the letter to Davenport. His mind should be wholly focused on his grandmother, ill and alone in the hospital. He should not be thinking about how seeing Bree rattled his longing for her loose.

When the seatbelt sign turned off, he shoved his computer into his satchel and stood in the aisle to stretch, but the second he moved toward the lavatory, the woman sitting two rows in front him cut him off and ducked into the stall before him. Of course, there was only one in business class.

"Shit."

"Sir, there are two other lavatories just behind the curtain if you don't want to wait," a flight attendant said.

She was the same attendant who greeted him when he got onboard. She was all legs and curves and loose curls with bright-pink lipstick. Her smile was impossibly wide, but it her expression that tipped him off. He suspected this was her best impression of flirting, but it just looked like she had a lazy eye.

"Uh, yeah. Thanks."

"Actually…" She winked and the right side of her mouth tugged into a wickedly scary grin. "If you want, I can walk you back."

Before Nadia, she would've been Shane's type for sure. She was right up his alley with the big rack and tight skirt. She was not at all what Beau wanted, though. He liked real women with real curves and real flaws. Just like the one behind the curtain.

Beau walked slowly behind the flight attendant to the lavatory door. Maybe she wasn't his type, but she could definitely help him out. It was one thing to get back there to use the restroom, but it also gave him an opportunity to see Bree.

"Is it close to the galley? I was hoping for a bottle of water."

"Absolutely! Tell you what. You use the lavatory, and I'll be waiting for you when you come out."

She parted the curtains and held one side open for Beau to

pass through. Her scary smile was back and became wider and creepier as she winked. Her spidery lashes flapped.

"Thanks a bunch."

He flashed her a tight smile and closed the door behind him. This was risky. He wanted to see Bree, but if she saw him with the flight attendant, things might not go over so well. He'd just have to keep a comfortable distance and make sure not to smile or laugh too much. All he wanted was a glimpse of Bree. He needed to see her eyes—if there was still love in them when she looked at him.

Beau relieved himself and flushed the toilet before washing and drying his hands. After a three count, he took a deep breath and opened the door. As planned, the flight attendant was waiting in the galley with a small bottle of water and her scary smile firmly in place.

"Here you are." She handed him the bottle and held onto it a second too long. *Perfect. She wants to talk.* "So, you're headed to the Windy City?"

Beau leaned against the far wall of the galley facing the coach seats, maintaining a few feet between them. He took his time opening the water and searching through the dark sea of heads. Only a few reading lights were on, but it was just enough to make out the faces.

"I'm...uh, going to see my grandmother."

At this, she swooned and purred rather loudly. It was then Beau saw Bree's head on the far right in an aisle seat a few rows from the back. A fresh wave of desire slammed into him.

"Aw. That's so sweet, going to see her for the holidays," the flight attendant cooed.

Beau stood taller and lifted his chin, but Bree didn't seem to notice him. Her eyes were down. She was reading a book with her elbow propped on the aisle armrest. When they were together, there wasn't a surface in their house that wasn't covered with books about everything under the sun—self-help, mystery, biographies, autobiographies, romance. She didn't discriminate as long as she was "feeding her brain," as she liked to call it. Books were research tools to widen her frame of reference for articles.

He squinted his eyes and bent a bit closer in Bree's direction, tilting his head hoping to make out the title. From so far away, he could only make out the colors red and green and a silhouette of some sort. Then he remembered what time of year it was and how her mother always sent her a Christmas romance novel to get into the season.

Beau felt a smile quivering over his lips and cleared his throat to keep it at bay. Laughter bubbled up inside him, and he just wanted to talk about it with Bree. It was their running joke that they could set a clock by the arrival of her mother's Christmas reading list. The Christmas romance was the one-week marker.

He missed this—their traditions and being with her. Bree was more than his fiancée. She was family.

It would definitely be too loud or too obvious, but he wanted to call to her or do something to catch her attention.

Maybe a stretch and yawn action, he thought. But then Miss Extra Helpful placed her hand on his forearm. "Is everything okay…I mean with, your grandmother? Is it hard to talk about?"

She seemed to confuse his silence with sadness, and now she was super close, practically in his face.

"I can get you some tissue if you want. I know how hard these things can be," she offered.

The irony of it was that her intuition was right on. His grandmother wasn't well, and he wasn't going back just to celebrate the holidays. He was flying back to be with her in the hospital where she was probably fighting for her life, and here he was concocting crazy plans to get a glimpse of the fiancée who'd walked out on him.

"Umm…" *Shit.* He raised his shoulders and attempted to wriggle loose from her clutches, but then he looked up. Right at that moment, while the leggy, tight-skirted flight attendant was fawning over him, his eyes snagged on the gaze of a wide-eyed Bree staring at the two of them.

It wasn't exactly love that he saw in her big, beautiful blue eyes when he looked at her, but there was definitely fire.

*A*ubrey jerked the book up higher and clamped her eyes shut. The poor, innocent book wrinkled around the edges under the strength of her death-grip. She was seeing more than red and green right now, and the shame of it all was that the book was actually starting to get to the good part.

She'd only set it down for a sec to pay for her drink and then she was going to get right back to it. The Jack Daniels had barely slid down her throat, and *wham!* Beau slipped through the curtain all distracting mouth and mischievous, sleepy gray eyes.

"Shit!" *Shit. Shit. Shit. Ugh! He saw me.*

She bit down on the inside of her cheek, unsure of what to do. He saw her, and still kept flirting with the cutesy flight attendant. *Should your skirt be that tight when you're supposed to be ready to save lives?*

A shiver coursed through her. She felt her forehead pinch. There was no denying he was attractive, which pissed her off almost as much as the fact that she didn't hate him like she thought she would when she saw him for the first time since they'd called off the engagement. She was both appalled and mesmerized.

The drawback was she could be as mad as she wanted to be, but her body responded to him. She sucked in a stark breath, fiery electricity coursing through her veins.

Heat crawled under her skin and settled there. She needed to do something, if only to throw up in her now-empty plastic cup full of holey ice. Better yet, she should probably eat the ice. Her blood was boiling. Hasty and utterly unladylike, she cocked the cup to her lips, and let two giant ice cubes slide into her mouth.

As she cooled and her nerves settled a teensy bit, she began to feel like a complete asswipe. She had nothing against the flight attendant. Really, she was lovely in an Angela Jolie, pouty-lipped vixen sort of way, despite her unfortunate creepy lashes. *Stunning.* It wasn't her fault Aubrey's ex was an even bigger asswipe, who couldn't sit still for two shakes. Really, the plane literally took off like ten minutes ago.

Ugh. *Complete asswipe.*

At her own risk, she lowered the book an inch and peeked over to the galley. Beau was still standing there all easy posture and eye contact, flashing the woman his dangerously, devastating smile. Of course, the flight attendant's blush deepened. A muscle ticked at Aubrey's jaw.

What should she do? Go over there and tell him to stop smiling? That was absurd, despite his nerve-shredding behavior.

She blew out a frustrated breath and sighed only to realize her suspiciously silent seatmate was staring at her, amused.

"Mix and Mingle All the Way, huh?"

Aubrey could feel her brow knitting together and her lips twisting. "Excuse me?"

"It's probably easier to read if you turn it right side up." He nodded to the book, which had apparently been upside down since she'd seen Beau schmoozing in the galley in front of God and everyone.

The realization was too much. She let the book fall to the tray table and deflated with a dramatic sigh on top of it. "This is not happening." Her arms dangled at her sides and she flitted a glance over to Chatty who was kind enough not to rub it in. There's no way Beau didn't see her pretending to be super engaged in a book.

"Don't worry. I don't think he can read at this distance."

Aubrey jolted upright. "You saw?"

"I'm somewhat of a expert at body language and people-watching. There's no need to be embarrassed that you were watching him. He may be over there with the stewardess, but his eyes have been on you the whole time. This tells me the woman does nothing for him as far as attraction goes." He paused for a moment and lifted his chin to look over the top of the chair in front of him, probably checking on Beau. "It's clear. He's gone. Was that the person you thought you recognized earlier?"

She plopped back against the seat and leaned slightly into the aisle. He *was* gone, and she was mortified. Aubrey nodded. "I'm so embarrassed."

Chatty cleared his throat and shifted in his seat to face her. For a brief moment, he seemed to study her movements and her apparently sluggish body language. "If you don't mind me asking, what happened between you two? It's obvious there's history here. I'm Pat, by the way. You can call me Paddy if you want. My friends do."

It could have been the alcohol or the insanity of Beau being on the plane, but hearing his real name was the most comical, hilarious thing in the world at the moment.

He isn't Chatty Cathy. He's Chatty Paddy.

A bout of giggles escaped Aubrey's mouth and she laughed hysterically, her chest rising and falling as she bent over, holding herself. When she finally came back down to earth, she still felt tickled on the inside, but she turned to Paddy.

"Are you sure you want to hear about my crazy life?" She winced and peeked at him with one eye. "It's really not that interesting. Typical maybe, but nothing you haven't heard before on *Oprah* or on some silly news outlet."

Paddy nodded. Apparently, he did want to know about her run of the mill loveless life.

"Okay, well if you insist. Here goes. We'd been together since high school. Back in Chicago, he proposed. I said yes, and I uprooted my life close by my family, which I didn't exactly mind. You'd understand if you met my mother, but that's another story.

Anyway, I moved to Las Vegas with him because his career was taking off. He was a broker at a financial firm, and I'm a freelance writer, so I can write anywhere. That was a big mistake because, naturally, it didn't work out. I was basically single without the benefit of cocktail-fused happy hours and wild sex. Sorry. TMI." Aubrey took a breath before continuing.

"I should have seen the signs that he was already in a relationship with his job and had an unhealthy obsession with climbing the corporate ladder. No promotion was ever big enough or enough money for him. He was never satisfied. So, at the end of the day…I left. He was never in a relationship with me. He was married to work and I didn't want to play second fiddle, considering I'd already compromised and left our hometown to be with him." She let out an exasperated breath. "That's it in a nutshell—all the high points at least."

The way Paddy looked at her, Aubrey wanted to shield her face with the book again. "What? Too much?" she asked.

"No," he said simply as if the vagueness of his answer covered the gambit of emotional responses. Reading him wasn't easy. His face was expressionless and wondering what he was thinking was killing her.

She was going through a hurricane of anger, annoyance, joy, sadness, fear, and humiliation. Still, she bit back her natural reaction to explode.

"Can you please say more? I can't take the silent treatment right now."

Really, the man has not stopped talking since we met at the gate and he chooses now to be cerebral and brooding?

He relaxed his shoulders and let the back of his head rest against the window as he stared at her. "Do you love him?"

Well, damn.

Aubrey's mouth fell open and she blinked. She was hesitant to tell him the truth, but what the heck did it matter if she told this guy? She was never going to see him again.

She nodded because saying it aloud would be too traumatizing.

He clasped his hands with the index fingers steepled up and chewed his bottom lip. "Ignore him. Pretend he doesn't exist. If he loves you, he'll make his way back to you."

In the back of her mind, she wanted to scream. *Uhh, stupid. Obviously, that hasn't worked for the last six months!* But then she thought more about it.

Out of sight, out of mind.

During the last six months, when she and Beau had not laid eyes on each other, she'd been sort of okay. Maybe it worked the other way around, too. Now that Aubrey was in Beau's sight, maybe he wouldn't be able to get her out of *his* mind.

LET IT SNOW

*W*hen the plane landed in Denver, and the crew opened the door, Beau was out of his seat and strolling into the gateway as soon as he could manage it. He was on a mission. The worst thing about red-eyes was no meal service. The layover in Denver was only forty-five minutes with a plane change, and he needed to grab something to eat quickly to tide him over. He also wanted to grab a magazine or a book to keep his mind occupied. It was obvious he wasn't going to be able to get any work done. Not with Bree on the same plane.

He hated how he couldn't stop looking over his shoulder and searching the storefronts as he walked through the terminal. Though he told himself he was just being mindful of his surroundings, there was no doubt in his mind what—*who*—he was looking for.

His stomach made a gurgling noise as if to remind him why he'd subjected himself to the cheery Christmas music and over-the-top decorations in the first place—the chance there might be eggnog milkshakes to go with a large fries. He'd be just fine skipping the whole season, but his grandmother had made sure to remind him of the meaning beyond the commercial holiday.

Slipping his phone from his coat pocket, Beau checked to make sure there were no new messages or updates regarding Grandma and sighed in relief when there were none. He was headed toward a small food court at the end of the terminal and happened to look up just as he passed a magazine stand close to the gate.

One quick glance, and there she was.

Beau bit back a grin as he watched Bree flipping through the pages of a fashion magazine. The sight of her still made his heart skip a beat. She could tell a whole story with only the movement of her hands and the slight sway of her willowy posture. He'd missed the sight of her parted lips. It made her look like she was in mid-conversation and might say the sweetest or sexiest thing without even meaning to. He licked his own lips as he watched her glide the pad of her finger over her bottom lip.

Holy...

The urge to be near her overtook him, but just as he was about to walk over to the bookshelves, the cashier glanced over at him.

"Can I help you with anything, sir?" The woman was in a head-to-toe elf costume and sounded about as merry as a funeral director. Of course, everyone standing around turned his or her attention to him, including Bree. She paused for just a moment, appeared to register his proximity to her, then immediately turned back to her magazine without so much as a smile or any acknowledgement he was there. *She saw him.*

He scrutinized her tense shoulders and lowered head. Her body language was closed off now, screaming for him to go away. *Oh, I see what we're doing here.* She was ignoring him, pretending he didn't exist, which Beau found mildly amusing. Even more, it felt like a challenge.

"I'm just looking, thanks," he replied casually to the cashier. He *was* just looking, though not at any cheeky souvenirs, Colorado T-shirts, or books on the bestseller list. His sights were firmly set on ruffling Bree's feathers. Odd that he was so set on capturing her attention, considering she was the one who packed her bags and left him. Still, if it was the last thing he did, he was going to make her face him.

But it was the game that excited him now.

From the small, refrigerated cooler, he grabbed a sandwich and a lemonade before slowly making his way over to the magazine stand where he closed the distance between them so he was standing just off to the left. She smelled like woman—toeing the edge of sweet and just the right amount of bitter. Beau stretched his arm over her shoulder and reached for the business magazines, lingering for a split second like he couldn't make up his mind which one he wanted to read. There couldn't have been more than four or five inches of space between their arms, and he was completely invading her personal space—an egregious pet-peeve offense he was well aware of, which was the plan.

She was getting better, though.

It took less than ten seconds for her eyes to shoot up. In his periphery, Beau watched as she stared, seemingly unblinking and unseeing at the colorful covers. The best part was the clench of her jaw jutting outward and the small vein visibly protruding from her temple. It was killing her, and *he* was loving every minute of it.

Come on. You know you want to say something.

As he returned the magazine to the shelf without the slightest glance at the pages, he bumped her arm ever so gently and… *jackpot!* Her foot began to tap, and she took her lip between her teeth like she was seeing red and wanted to murder him on principle alone. She might have, if she hadn't sensed it was exactly the reaction he was prodding for.

A teensy laugh rumbled through Beau. He was tickled at this comedy of errors. "Pardon me," he muttered just to get her blood really boiling.

It wouldn't be long.

Instead of the explosion he was hoping for, Bree simply

replaced the copy she was holding on the shelf, grabbed another one, and plodded over to the cashier.

This is my chance.

Beau leapt into action as she went for the Snickers bar all the way at the back of the row—another little habit of hers, thinking less people were likely to touch the items stocked in the back. Her fingers grazed the top, but he was quicker. Right out of her grasp, he nabbed it, and *voilà. Success.*

"What the fuck is your problem? Do you really need attention that badly?"

"Oh," Beau leaned back feigning surprise to see her. "Hi, Bree… Aubrey. How are you?" The dip between his brows deepened as he tried not to laugh aloud. "It's good to see you."

Bree rolled her eyes and folded her arms. "Seriously? Don't be an asshole. You saw me about to grab that Snickers and you took it first on purpose."

He had her right where he wanted her. "I'm sorry. I don't know what you're talking about. I was simply looking to satisfy a craving. Besides, if anyone is being rude, it's you. You clearly saw me and said nothing. Just because you left me doesn't mean we can't be friends."

At his own risk, he flashed her a shaky smile.

"I'll say this much. You don't waste any time," she replied. "Looked like you were enjoying your business class amenities and taking full advantage of the flight attendants." Her stare was pointed and her words were not minced. It *was* fire he'd seen in her eyes when she was watching him talking in the galley.

She's jealous.

"Let's not confuse things. You left me without even the courtesy of a good explanation."

Bree's eyes widened with indignation then narrowed like she might strangle him. He thought she might laugh, but she opened her mouth, a flush reddening her cheeks, before she forced her lips closed with apparent resolution not to stoop to Beau's level.

She pivoted away from him, but then turned back with that same fire blazing in her eyes.

"I...can't do this." The words struggled out and died on her tongue as she exhaled a chest full of steam. There was so much more she wanted to say, but she was holding back. *Why?* "I can't pretend we're just old friends running into each other over the holiday season. This isn't some sappy Christmas meet-cute in a movie. I walked out on you for a *damn* good reason." She peeked up through her lashes at him, sniffling, her voice thick with emotion. "Because we both know you were in a committed relationship with your job long before I left my key on the entry table."

Her eyes were glossy. Tears sat on the rim of her eyes and as she swallowed, allowing her chin to drop to her chest. The sight of her, broken like this, stabbed at Beau's heart. In a momentary lapse of judgment, he reached for her hand and she pulled it back.

"Don't. I'm okay."

She shook her head and eyed the few onlookers who'd gathered since his attempt to be playful. He knew she wasn't okay. Nothing about this moment, this meeting after all these months, felt right. They were supposed to be together, starting a life and following their plan. The two of them were going to beat the odds, but here they were, two strangers in passing.

"I'm sorry. I didn't mean to—"

"I know." She lifted her chin without meeting his gaze and said, "Just...go away, Beau."

He was fully prepared to respect her wishes and pretend, as long as it meant never again seeing the pained expression in her eyes or the way her lower lip pursed and quivered as she held back.

He nodded and widened the distance between them in the line. She placed another chocolate bar, the magazine, a banana, and an orange juice on the counter.

"That'll be eleven twenty-five please."

"Oh, okay. Just let me…" Bree fished three ones and a five from her wallet and began scrounging coins from the bottom of her purse. "It seems I'm a little short. Can I put the juice back?"

One would think a person who wears an elf costume with pointed ears would have a lighter attitude or a sense of holiday spirit, but the cashier huffed loudly like it would kill her to remove an item from the order. Dramatically, with one hand on her hip, she stabbed at the keys and shot Bree an exasperated, raised-brow, pursed-lip expression before announcing the new total. "Nine dollars and eight cents" she seethed.

"Here, try my card." Bree bit her lip and glanced around apologetically at the people in line behind them. "I'm sorry."

That's when Miss Customer Service of the Year informed her that her card was declined. "You have enough for the banana and the chocolate bar," she said with more annoyance bleeding into her tone. It was too much for Beau to watch.

He pulled out a twenty and slapped it on the counter. "Merry Christmas…" He leaned in and cocked his head to read her bright red nametag. "…*Joy*. Hope you're having a *joyful* holiday. I'd like to pay for this lady's order along with my sandwich and lemonade here, if you don't mind." He raised his brows as he set his items on the counter along with Bree's, daring the woman to say one more unkind word.

They all stood there in silence while the woman rang them up and when the cash drawer popped open, Beau retrieved his change. "Thank you, *Joy*. I hope the rest of your day goes better." Then he turned to Bree. "Happy Holidays to you. I'm sorry to have bothered you. I won't do it again." Before she could say a word in response, he walked away.

*A*ubrey watched Beau leave the magazine stand and round the corner back toward the gate. If she weren't in a public place on high alert for terrorists, and already mortified beyond belief, she would have screamed to the top of her lungs and thrown herself onto the floor in a fit. God, she wanted to hate Beau for being a smug, charming asshole who made friends with flirty flight attendants and angry elves. She wanted to yell at him for riling her up with stupid antics and making her feel like some demure lady who needed rescuing. Even more, she wanted to strangle him for being so goddamned adorably boyish and gorgeous while he did it.

Was it possible he was taller? He was so tall and handsome, with dark brown hair and heavy dark brows over bright gray eyes. She missed his coy, upturned lips. They were sinfully beautiful and pouty, and had a way of making her feel naked when he licked them even while she wore all these layers of clothing.

"Ugh." She grunted and wringed her fingers just as the guy with giant headphones who was standing behind Beau in line walked past. "I'm sorry."

She was starting to annoy *herself* with her constant apologizing. She'd made a scene ordering Beau to go away, and not even two seconds later, she needed him to come in with all of his money to save the day. What. The. Heck?

Why am I so on edge?

Strike that. Aubrey knew exactly why she was bent out of shape, and the sooner she got out of this godforsaken airport, onto the plane to finish her article, and back to Chicago, she would be rid of Beau and back to her normal life—whatever that was.

There was no way in hell she was going to owe him money, though. After all they'd been through, she knew money *was* the root of all evil—or at least to their breakup. If he hadn't been working a million hours a week to earn obscene amounts of money, he would have been home to eat dinner at the table, binge-watch movies and shows, or for them to fall asleep together. She could have taken her time making love to him, feeling him moving inside her the way they used to. She loved the way they'd felt like one person living in two bodies. Was that so much to ask? Apparently, it was because he chose work, money, and snazzy business class flights over everything that meant anything to her.

"Not on your life, Redgrave."

She marched through the terminal until she reached the gate and scanned the seats, searching for Beau. When she spotted him, she about stomped her way over and loomed in front of him aggressively.

"Just so you know, I'm not broke. It's Friday and I get paid today. As soon as my paycheck hits my account, I'll send you your money. I don't want to owe you anything," she said.

"It's fine, really. Just think of it as spreading holiday cheer." He tilted his head and flashed her that disarmingly hot lopsided grin that he knew she loved. Although, now, the smugness behind it crawled under her skin and left Aubrey seething mad.

She could feel the vein at her temple twitch as she sighed. "Cut the shit, Beau. I know you don't like the Christmas holiday, so don't act like you're some benevolent do-gooder here to save me. Every cent will be in your account in a few hours, so don't think you did me any favors. I'm doing fine, and I don't need rescuing."

Beau raised his hands in mock defense, a smile toying at his lips. "Okay. Fine with me, but I don't mind paying for you."

Typical. Everything was always about money with him. His ability to pay for himself and others, like life was just an endless party. He always got the next round of drinks, or the paid the check, or...was able to buy airport snacks for the poor girl whose card was declined for eleven bucks.

"I don't *need* you to pay for me." Aubrey shot him a look that she hoped read *don't push it.* She took a deep breath that was meant to be cleansing, but failed epically, turned on her heel, and dragged her feet toward an empty seat on the far side of the gate by the window.

She was still fuming mad as she looked outside. The mountains in the distance were barely visible. It was a winter wonderland of snow flurries and white draped over every surface. The wind whipped and whirled, and with the Christmas music playing in the background, she *almost* wished she was already home with Mom, Dad, and Matt. Anywhere was better than here, especially with Beau sitting across the gate.

Casually, she peeked over to where he was seated and quickly tore her gaze away when she saw that he was staring at her.

God, get me out of this airport before I slide all the way back to square one.

Aubrey checked her watched before flitting a glance over to the gate agents. They were probably going to start the boarding any minute. It wasn't enough time to take out her computer to write, but ironically, Beau paid for just the thing she needed to keep her mind off of him.

The day hadn't been all bad. Aubrey still couldn't believe the call she'd received that morning from a client telling her about Virage magazine—the only Chicago-based fashion magazine that mattered. They were hiring, and not only was Aubrey being considered, but whatever magical piece she'd come up with was going straight to the top of the pile.

An assistant editor position becoming available at Virage was like some sort of otherworldly, blue-moon miracle people in the fashion industry prayed for but basically knew would never come to pass. It was the NBA or major league for fashion writers. Applicants could play the game, read every issue, and submit their resumes regularly, but the likelihood of working with editor-in-chief, Gena Detrich, was a pipe dream for most. Aubrey still considered it a long shot, even after a client, who she freelanced for back in September, slipped her name to Gena in conversation at an after-party during fashion week. Aubrey might not be a shoo-in, but getting this article written and turned in by Monday would certainly improve her chances.

To get started, though, she needed to know everything she could find out about Gena Detrich, starting with the woman's life history and the basics on the editor's page in the holiday issue of Virage.

Aubrey flipped through the first few pages, and there was Gena, impeccably dressed, with her arms folded across her chest like a boss. She had shoulder-length, shiny, jet-black hair that framed impossibly high cheekbones and deep-set, piercing blue eyes. Aubrey could practically hear the angels sing when looking at this badass.

In the next moment, Aubrey wished she could plead with the angels for deliverance. Then, the sharply dressed gate agent propped his elbows on the counter to make an announcement. His voice cracked over the PA.

"We are sorry to announce that Omega Air flight 1225 has been delayed for two to three hours due to weather conditions. Hopefully, things will return to normal once the weather lets up, but in the meantime, we apologize for any inconvenience."

A collective sigh erupted over the gate and people groaned over Nat King Cole crooning about chestnuts roasting on an open fire. Next began the chatter about missing flight connections and reimbursements. *What are we supposed to do now? Don't you know how late it is? It's the holidays!*

All were valid points, though misdirected. It was not as if the gate agent was in cahoots with Mother Nature and knew exactly when the light snow might morph into a blizzard and delay the flight. There was no sense in getting mad. Aubrey didn't mind a few more hours away from her mom. It was the stuck-in-an-airport-with-Beau conundrum that left her feeling unhinged.

Since she was apparently a sadist, she risked looking over at him. Thankfully, he wasn't staring back. He was on his phone.

"Water?"

Aubrey turned to find the gate agent offering her a water bottle. She looked around to see other airline employees following suit, likely trying to ease the passengers' troubles. "Oh, thank you," she said.

As he passed by, Aubrey looked over at Beau again. This time he packed up, shouldered his duffle, and dragged his suitcase straight toward her. She could feel her eyes go wide and her heart began racing. As much as she tried, her leg would not stop tapping, so she clamped her free hand down on it and lowered her eyes, trying to look busy reading the magazine. She couldn't focus in on any words on the page.

The second he reached her, he wasted no time. "Listen, I know you're still mad and I said I wouldn't bother you, but I'm pretty certain this storm is only going to get worse. It's two thirty in the morning, and I'm tired. I've got a room reserved at the Wooldridge Hotel right here at the airport, and there's another flight this afternoon. So, if you want, you can stay with me. I got two queen beds just in case you said yes. Room 611."

Beau stood there for a second and all Aubrey wanted to do was say yes, go back to his hotel room with him and forget about the last six months. She wanted to tell him that nothing else mattered except that they were together. But, the pain she'd been through all these years, waiting and wishing he'd put her first, rose up in her throat like bile. She couldn't be a convenient choice anymore, no matter how much her body pulsed, pricked, and tingled just being near him.

Really, the man was sinfully good looking.

She blinked up at him, her mouth open and breathless as her heart pounded in her ears. Her shoulders were nearly up to her ears and she felt like she was floating, stuck in a magnetic field being drawn to him. She blinked again, yanking herself from his trance.

Don't fall for it.

"I…uh. Um…no," she rasped, her voice barely above a whisper. She shook her head and tore her gaze away. "Thanks, though. That's really kind of you."

Beau didn't wait around while she contemplated her response, weighing the pros and cons the way she always did when a choice presented itself. He turned and quickly strode away, rolling his suitcase behind him. His form faded into the distance while her jaw still hung to the floor.

LAST CHRISTMAS

From the back of the cab, Beau caught sight of the hotel up ahead on the right. He'd stayed at the Wooldridge many times for business and once or twice during visits with his grandmother when she wasn't busy with church events. He knew most of the staff by name and often chatted at registration for a few minutes before heading up to his room. Tonight, though, he just wanted to grab his key and duck into the elevator with as little human contact as possible. He wanted to be alone, and he would be. Bree had made sure of it.

During the drive, Beau had called to check on his grandmother, and hearing that she was stable and doing well eased his worries a bit. She was asking for him, though, and his urgency to get to her increased. If anyone could steer him in the right direction regarding Bree, it was Grandma. She was his only family, and her advice came simply and effortlessly. For the time being, he'd have to settle for mediocre advice from Shane.

"Right here is fine, thanks," he said. He paid the cabby and stepped out into the chilled darkness of the early-morning hours. He slipped out his phone and tapped Shane's name. Beau needed to let him know where he was, but he could also use the call to minimize his interactions with the staff.

"Hey."

Apparently, Shane was an asshole no matter the hour. "Calm down with all that bass this early in the morning," Shane said groggily. "Ladies can't get enough of all that deep baritone shit. Where are you?" Beau could hear Nadia in the background asking if everything was all right. "Yeah, it's just Beau," Shane said. "He's…what *are* you doing?"

"Just so you know, I am worried about one lady in particular. My grandmother is not well. I'm on my way back to Chicago, but since it was so last-minute, I had to take the red-eye with a connection out of Denver. Of course, the snow delayed the flight, so I'm in Denver until the next flight this afternoon."

The only plus to strolling into a hotel at this hour was there were no lines, and, fortunately, no one he recognized on the late shift. Beau walked straight up to the registration desk and nodded at the young woman behind the counter. Sandwiching the phone between his ear and shoulder, he handed her his ID and credit card. "I just called a short while ago. It's under Redgrave," he whispered.

"Yes, I have it here," she said tapping her computer keyboard. She retrieved a few documents from the printer and returned with the room key. "You're all set."

Beau thanked her and turned toward the elevator, listening to Shane. The line was silent for a bit before he spoke. "Ah, man. I'm really sorry," Shane said. "Is she…going to be okay? Do you know what's wrong with her?"

Beau pressed the button for the sixth floor and waited until the door closed behind him before speaking.

"The doctor couldn't say much, but it's to do with her diabetes —low blood sugar. It happens, but I called the hospital right before I called you. The most recent report shows she's doing fine

—stable and alert. She's still asking for me, and I need to be there, but—"

"No, yeah. I totally get it," Shane replied. "Go to her. She's your family. I'll hold everything down in the office. I've got you. Plus, no one really does anything in December. Everyone's already talking about first quarter goals and shit, so just go…be there for her."

Beau took a deep breath and evened his tone, raking his hand through his hair. He couldn't disconnect without telling Shane about running into Bree. Shane was going to find out eventually and give him shit for it, and, also, Beau felt like he might explode if he didn't tell someone.

"There's something else…" he trailed off, the words dying on his tongue. *Shit.*

"Whatever it is, I'm here for you."

His heart pummeled his chest and he felt like his ribs might break as he swallowed and tried to imagine what Shane would say. He and Nadia were no longer just Beau's friends. They were his and Bree's friends together. They'd done the double date thing and planned to live on the same block and raise families together. There was talk of their unborn children one day playing soccer or softball team together. They'd be in the same karate classes because their kids weren't going to take shit from other little snotty-nosed ankle-biters. Somehow, Beau had messed it all up. He'd let Bree get away.

"I saw her."

Beau could tell Shane knew exactly who he was talking about without even saying her name. It was barely audible, but he heard Shane release a tiny gasp and then the swish of a hand over the phone as he attempted to muffle the line. "He saw Bree," Shane was telling Nadia.

Beau imagined the two of them sitting up ramrod straight in bed freaking out because they knew what it meant.

I don't know how I feel anymore. I'll know when I see her.

It felt like just yesterday, and it also felt like twenty years ago. She'd walked out and he'd hoped, prayed, and wished she'd return, but she never did. The elevator doors opened, and as Beau dragged his feet down the hall toward his room, his mind went to his mother.

Her face was so young. With her dark, olive skin and long, chestnut hair she'd seemed like a goddess to Beau. She was soft-spoken and gentle with him, like she thought he might break. "I'll be back before you know it, and then it'll be just us—two peas in a pod." She peppered a velvet kiss on his cheek. "You and me. I promise."

"Did you talk to her?" Shane asked, snapping Beau back to the present. "Beau? Are you good, man? What did she say?"

He told Shane about seeing Bree in the line at the gate in Vegas and how it rattled something loose inside of him—how seeing her after a long absence felt like a homecoming. He also told him about the plane, the flight attendant, the layover in Denver, and the way she'd ignored him at the magazine stand.

Beau inserted his room key and let his bags falls to his sides, leaning on the doorframe as he wrapped up the story with the weather delay and how he'd offered to let Bree to stay with him in the hotel.

"She didn't come," Shane said. It was a statement, not a question.

Hearing the words spoken back to him, Beau couldn't down-play it. Even in its most watered down form, it was the truth glaring back at him. *She doesn't love me anymore.*

It really was over.

"That's about the size of it." He slipped out of his coat and laid it on the chair in the far corner of the room by the window. His body felt heavy, and his eyes were open, but he wasn't looking at anything in particular. He blinked and gave a noncommittal nod. "I guess... I just thought that when we saw each other again, we'd both realize it was mistake. We'd apologize to each other because we'd know without a doubt that apart, we're were only half a person."

He cleared his throat and pinched the bridge of his nose. "I just need to—"

"Have you called Davenport?"

"No, why—"

"Don't. I've gotta be honest here," Shane began. "You're fucking up. I knew it was going to come to this, but I thought you'd have your shit together by now." He sighed, but seemed to resolve himself to continue with his spiel. "Look, I know we said one of us needed to make it to the top, and I know you'll get the position if you want it, but where are you trying to go? When's it ever going to be high enough?"

Beau couldn't believe his ears.

"You and Bree...you had something good," Shane continued. "I know you don't want to hear this from me, but you're going to have to choose. Not about everything in your life, but about her, definitely. You need to be absolutely sure that you're okay being without her."

No, Beau wasn't sure about that. He was not the one who decided to end their relationship, but after seeing her today, he knew he wanted her back. Nothing would ever feel right without her. Beau's eyes widened and his fingers danced at his sides. He was antsy and fired up, like he needed to take action.

"What should I do?" The words came out tentative and unsure, breathless.

"The way I see it, you have two choices. You can go back to the airport, find her, and tell her you can't live without her. Or, you can wait. See if she shows up. If she doesn't, let it go for good. It's as simple as that."

The choice hung there in the air, jagged and sharp. Beau knew that leaving her be would cut him to the quick, but did he have a choice? Bree made it clear how she felt at the airport. With every attempt he'd made to break the ice, she ignored him and shut him down.

Beau ended his call with Shane but promised to keep him abreast of how things turned out. Then, he went about the task of settling in the room. Beau toed off his shoes, allowing his feet to sink into the plush carpet. As he unbuttoned his shirt, he pressed the button on the phone to dial room service. The day had taken a toll on him. His mind and body were exhausted.

He plopped down on the edge of the bed closest to the door, flicked on the television, and stared absently at the screen. His mind was a breeding ground for idle thoughts. He replayed every moment since he'd laid eyes on Bree in the airport, lingering on one moment in particular.

I'm doing fine, and I don't need rescuing.

Her words echoed in the back of his mind. She'd made the decision for him. She was doing fine without him, and now he needed to accept it.

Beau wouldn't rescue her. He wouldn't be going back to the airport to find her and confess his feelings. As much as he hated it, he knew there was nothing left to do but wait.

The elevator doors opened, and Aubrey set her shoulders back and lifted her chin. Somehow, in all of her resolve to stand her ground and prove she wasn't second fiddle, she knew she'd end up right where she was, on the sixth floor of the Wooldridge Hotel, unable to move her feet.

The long, bright hallway seemed to go on for miles. Every few doors, ornate golden sconces and decorative mirrors broke up the endless, stenciled jade and beige floral print wallpaper, marking how far she had to go. She eyed the numbers on the first door on her right as she managed to take a step. *601.*

You can do this.

She slipped her hand into her coat pocket and found the small hole, running her finger over the frayed fabric. She closed her eyes, took three deep calming breaths, and slowly opened her eyes again.

"What am I doing? *Why* did I come here?"

Her nerves were rattled.

Aubrey knew the partial answer to her question. Much to her chagrin, shortly after Beau left her with her jaw still on the floor, Chatty Paddy found her and proceeded to complete an actuarial risk analysis and the projected life span of the first five people to walk past them based on their shoes. It was either their soles or her soul, so here she was, clawing her way toward Beau's door.

When she was two rooms from his, she could see the number 611 in the distance, but she physically could not lift her feet. Even they knew she shouldn't be there. She closed her eyes and leaned her forehead onto the hard coolness of the wall. For a split second, banging it a few times didn't seem like the worst idea.

Breathe. It's only Beau, and it's a place to kick off my shoes for a few hours...and pee.

Aubrey took a deep breath and tried to still her body, but all she could think of was running water and oceans and—

"Are you locked out?" A voice from behind her snapped her out of her trance and almost scared the pee right out of her. "I can call down to registration or let one of the maids know for you if you want. The inflection in the man's voice was chipper, a high-pitched, singsong tone underneath the sound of metal and wheels rolling.

"I...I'm okay, thanks," Aubrey said, turning. "I was just stopping to catch my breath."

The guy pushed a room service cart carrying a bottle of water, a glass of milk, and a covered plate of what smelled like warm, freshly baked, chocolate chip cookies and... She sniffed. *Croissants.* Her stomach gurgled as she swallowed back her hunger. The orange juice, banana, and candy bar were not going to cut it much longer. "Thanks, though."

He shot her a curious stare. His eyes traveled from her boots to her light blazer before he met her gaze. "Sure. Just to let you know, the weather's getting pretty bad outside. If you were planning on going back out there, you might want to wait for a while. It's supposed to be brutal tonight."

"Ah. Gotcha." She nodded far too long not to arouse suspicions about what she was doing loitering in a hotel, but what was she going to do? She couldn't exactly move at the moment, and watching the water slosh around in the bottle on the cart as he pushed it only made things worse. She crossed one foot in front of the other and bent down to pretend like she was wiping something off of her boot. She was really trying to squeeze her bladder into submission. *Don't pee. Don't pee.*

Only when he was far enough down the hall, knocking on a door, did she right herself. He'd narrowly missed seeing a golden shower. It was then that she noticed the door number.

611. *Shit.*

Her pulsed quickened, and a rising tide of panic crashed down on her as her fight or flight instincts revved in the direction of flight. With her heart knocking, she waddled as carefully and as quickly as she could back toward the elevator.

"Bree?" *Too late.*

Aubrey squeezed her thighs together. At the desperate tone in his voice, the urge to pee subsided and was replaced by a totally different need for relief. She could feel the crease between her brows trenching. Her stomach did a little flip, and her heart pounded against her chest. *Why did I come here?*

When she didn't move or turn to meet his gaze, Beau called her name again. "Bree?"

Her name on his tongue never sounded sweeter, but Lord, if she stepped foot into his room, she was a goner. If there was one thing the man was good at, it was definitely sex—otherworldly, carnal, toe-tingling, eight-hour sleep sex.

"Bree, it's fine. I got the double beds, so…" *Great.* Now, not one, but two beds to really test her restraint. The devil's creativity was totally underrated.

But, there's also a toilet. Dammit.

Aubrey pivoted toward him in slow motion with her lips parted. Her heart slowed to a sluggish thud in her ears as she registered the wistful stare adorably affixed to his beautiful face. A lump formed in her throat as she caught a brief glimpse of the boy she'd planned to marry so long ago. He was all man now.

A smile tugged around the edges of her mouth. "Hey."

He lifted an accusatory brow. *He knows you were chickening out.*

The simultaneous realization made them both laugh because she was truly so busted. She wasn't going to deny it, even if half her body was still hedged to the elevator. If she really wanted to, she could probably still make a break for it, but the sight of Beau looking like a delicious snack as he very sexily pulled the corner of his lip between his teeth made Aubrey's heart skip around in her chest.

Involuntarily, her body moved a step closer. Like a magnet she was drawn to him.

Beau gave her his patented easygoing, sex god look then turned his attention to the guy from room service. He signed the receipt in the leather check presenter and let the guy roll the cart past him into the room. Then he returned the full weight of his focus to Aubrey. He had a carefree posture and a lopsided grin as he studied her.

Dammit if she could just keep still.

The urge to go was back in full force. "Fine. I'm coming in, but I have to pee." Aubrey shrugged and rolled her eyes as she bit back a laugh at her ridiculous dilemma.

His smile grew, and his blush deepened. A fresh wave of desire slammed into her. "I thought I noticed the tail-end of an emergency status dance." His shoulders shook as silent laughter rumbled over him.

It wasn't until the door clicked shut behind them that Aubrey realized what she'd done.

"This is…" She trailed off, scanning her surroundings. The suite was beyond luxurious, with floor-length windows overlooking the Mile-High City. The irony and sexual innuendo was not lost on her at all. The sleek, modern furniture was draped in warm textures and accented with pops of red. The suite was downright romantic. When they were together, Aubrey dreamed of Beau whisking her away on a sexy little getaway to just this type of place. Through the glass-paneled French doors leading to the master suite she saw two formidably sized beds dressed to the nines in billowing white linen clouds. If Aubrey wasn't trying to act breezy and carefree, she might have taken a running start, jumped, and let herself land in the middle of one of them. She realized that even in this tempting environment, they were on neutral territory. Neither one of them had any friends or family in Denver. There was nowhere to run. "It's beautiful," she managed.

It's only for a few hours. Just…make the best of it.

She rubbed her hands together, thankful for the central heating and the fact that she wouldn't be stuck at the airport getting her ears talked off while she fought to stay awake.

As Beau took her coat and bags and sat them near the window on the far wall facing the street, her heart flooded with homesickness. He was her world for so long. She was warm and way too comfortable being so close to him. He crossed the floor back toward her and stopped just a whisper away.

"Do you need anything?"

Her mind snagged on all the possible answers to that question running through her mind. *Chocolate chip cookies. Hot Mile-High City sex. You…*

"No." *Yes.*

"You sure?" Beau dragged his bottom lip between his teeth and stared into her—she could read his real questions in his expression. *Are you sure you don't want to talk about us? Are you sure we shouldn't rethink the last torturous six months? Do you want to give it another go, starting tonight in one of those two inviting beds?*

His familiar sunshine and soap scent tickled her nose and her insides felt like they were attached to a drawstring low in her belly which he'd pulled tight. Aubrey wanted to scream yes to each of the questions in his eyes, but the word lodged in her throat along with everything else she'd compromised. She was tired of being the flexible one, the one Beau and everyone in her family knew would blink first.

If you want me back, Beau Redgrave, it's going to take more than a cocky half smile and a pair of twinkling eyes.

With wide, round eyes, Aubrey met his disarmingly sexy, mischievous ones. Hers burned and watered, but she didn't blink.

"Bathroom?" It came out as a question. The high inflection on "room" hung out there like a suggestion.

She asked, not because she needed to go so badly anymore, but because she couldn't just stand there feeling awkward and unsure of what to do with herself around Beau. He looked wide-eyed, hopeful, and sweet. It would be way too easy and too natural to slide back into old habits…too easy to remember how much she loved him.

Aubrey pivoted and walked toward the door of the en suite bathroom just beyond the bed on the left and promptly locked it behind her. She was breathless and boneless. She'd walked so fast she barely registered her surroundings. The echo of the television crept beneath the door and the sound of Christmas music pinballed off the tile.

Even without seeing the screen, Aubrey knew the movie like the back of her hand. She'd watched it about one million times. Pathetically, sometimes she watched it when it wasn't the holidays. She could see Kate Winslet blubbering and sobbing as she paced her kitchen carrying around the weight of her broken heart. A somber version of "Have Yourself a Merry Little Christmas" played in the background while Kate considered the benefits of gas inhalation during a momentary low point.

Accepting an invitation back to Beau's hotel room was far from huffing gas from the stove, but tonight felt like Aubrey's low point.

"You're going to be in heaven when you come out here," Beau yelled from the other room. She could hear the sound of metal clanking and the splash of liquid being poured. "They've been playing these movies all day on every channel apparently. It's some kind of countdown marathon, and your favorite is on right now. Oh, and I've got warm chocolate chip cookies."

Despite herself, Aubrey let her weight sink against the doorframe and smiled. Things between them didn't work out the way she'd hoped, but maybe going somewhere new and doing something completely out of her comfort zone would was just what she needed.

She stared at her reflection in the mirror and slowly pulled the elastic band from her hair, letting her auburn strands fall loose over her shoulders. Her cheeks were still bright pink. They hadn't yet thawed from the chilly December air. For the first time in a long while, when she saw herself in the mirror, she recognized herself and was encouraged to see a small spark in her lively blue eyes and a colorful glow of hope shimmering on her skin. The smattering of freckles over the bridge of her nose danced in the fluorescent light.

Something like fire blazed inside her.

"I'll be right out."

She took a deep breath and toed off her boots. Her heart knocked and her skin pulsed.

Her smile spread and curled up on one side. Either this idea brewing in her head was brilliant, or she was completely losing her shit, but at the moment, she didn't want to think. She didn't want to think about what it meant to come to Beau's hotel, or what compromises she may or may not make. She didn't want to think about the holidays or Matt's engagement party. She wanted to remember what she was missing.

A few minutes later, Aubrey let her panties fall to the floor alongside the rest of her clothes and she wrapped her fingers around the doorknob. Tonight, she just wanted to live in the moment and think about the consequences later.

ALL I WANT FOR CHRISTMAS
IS YOU

Beau ripped open the packet of hot chocolate, emptied it into the mugs and poured hot water over the top. He was still stirring when he heard the bathroom door open with a whoosh.

"Everything come out all right?" he joked, feeling particularly jovial. His spirits couldn't have been higher at the moment. Bree had come back to the hotel and back into his life. She'd shown up, which meant there was still hope, and he couldn't deny the relief he felt when he'd seen her in the hall.

"I think so," she said, her voice low, laughter bleeding into it. "I'm going to wait for you in here, funny guy."

"Okay. Make yourself comfortable while I finish up. I saw you had your laptop with you. It's fine if you want to plug in and write. What are you working on lately?"

"I'm finally submitting to Virage."

Beau paused before he spoke. Bree had been considering applying for years and talked herself out of it just as long. He was happy for her, but he also knew her writing was good enough to get the job—a position a long way from Vegas.

"Congratulations. You deserve this," he said.

He was still busying himself with their little late-night snack, so he didn't turn to her. Instead, he opened a teensy cup of French vanilla creamer and added it to their cups. It was the next-best thing to marshmallows or whipped cream—perfect to go with the cookies and the movie marathon. It was small, but Beau wanted everything to be perfect for Bree.

The air was warm and sweet and made him feel childish happiness.

Once the tray was filled with the cookies and mugs, he slowly lifted it, careful not to spill as he turned and inched toward the bedroom.

Then he saw Bree lying naked in a cloud of sheets and blankets, and he nearly lost his mind and his motor skills.

"Don't drop the cookies," she said, biting her bottom lip.

"Bree—"

"Don't talk. Just put the tray down and come over here," she whispered, her voice thick with emotion. "I just want to be with you tonight."

Beau's heart stuttered in his chest. He swallowed and raked a hand through his hair, unable to tear his gaze away from the curves of her body. There was no question he wanted Bree. He just didn't want her to think this was why he'd asked her back to the hotel. He'd wanted to be there for her in her time of need, not as a rescuer, as she put it, but as the man who would turn the world upside down to make things right between them again. Inviting her to stay was his way of showing what was important to her was important to him. She could count on him.

"I, uh…"

Her cheeks reddened and the corners of her eyes narrowed into a smile. "There's no sense in denying you want this, too. I'm guessing by the sizeable hard-on struggling against your jeans, your body is as ready as mine."

Beau lowered his chin to laugh before lifting it again and meeting her eyes. "Of course. I want nothing more. It's just, I didn't ask you here for this. Don't get me wrong, it's a lovely surprise, but..." he trailed off unsure how far to take this confession. He didn't want to risk ruining things again. He needed to tread lightly, but the second he registered the expression on her face and the way her shoulders slumped, he wished he could take it all back.

In a blur of quick movements and white sheets, Bree jolted upright and wrapped herself in them.

Almost instantly, regret flared in Beau's gut as he rushed to her side and gathered her into his arms. "I didn't mean it like—" The words skidded on his tongue. He sounded frantic and worried.

"How did you mean it then?" she cut him off.

His face grew hot at the raw emotion in her voice, but he was still adjusting to the feel of her warmth and the softness of her skin against his. She felt like home.

"It's okay if you don't want me anymore," she said. "I was stupid to come here, get undressed, and think having sex with you one more time was going to make me feel something again. I know you've probably moved on." She squeezed her eyes closed and her body stiffened in his arms.

"I love you," Beau rasped. He said the words before he could overthink it and she quieted. He buried his face into her hair and into her neck. "I've always loved you. There's no one else. These last six months, I've missed you terribly. I thought you'd come back, and when I saw you today, I knew I couldn't keep pretending I'm okay without you. I can change. I can work less. I can be the man you need me to be."

Bree twisted in his embrace until they were face to face. She was sniffling and her eyes were puffy and red, but she was smiling.

"I do. I love you, Aubrey Green." A shiver coursed through him and it shook him to the core.

Slowly, he placed both of his hands on the soft curves of her cheeks and brushed his lips over hers. She tasted of sweet mint and chocolate, but she looked like sin. As he deepened the kiss, she let the sheets fall and Beau felt the warmth coming off her skin. Through his shirt, he felt her nipples harden. Then she pressed her pelvis to his cock.

In a move that almost sent Beau over the edge, Bree dipped the pads of her fingers beneath the band of his pants and boxer briefs. His full length awaited her. Heat seared through him, and he parted his lips in a pleasured gasp before taking hers between his teeth and gently biting.

"Fuck." He breathed the word through a shallow breath. "I want you."

Bree looked up at him over her brow. There was heat and mischief mixed with a little determination in her eyes. Without saying a word, she gripped the hem of his shirt with both hands and waited for him to lift his arms over his head. Slowly and torturously, she removed the shirt, leaving blazing, scraping trails up his chest with her fingernails as she did. Then, she lowered herself onto the bed and proceeded to unzip his pants, working them, along with his boxer briefs down his hips and to the floor.

When she was finished, she scooted back and leaned on her elbows with her legs hanging open, studying him. "I want you, too."

Beau twined their fingers together and pinned her hands over her head as he positioned himself between her legs. With his knees, he pried her legs further apart and pressed the head of his cock at the juncture between her thighs. "Holy... Yes." She was already wet for him, but as he gently glided the tip inside, she let out a sharp cry of satisfaction. He thrust the full length inside her, then settled into a steady rhythm.

He crawled his fingers down to her breasts and lowered his head to suckle them one at time as she arched beneath him.

"Oh my God, yes. Please don't stop." She moaned. "Keep going. I'm coming."

"Me too," Beau said, feeling his cock tighten and harden.

Her breathing came out in pants and grunts as she met each hard, fast push and Beau was savoring the feel of every touch. She was clinging to his body with her head back and her mouth open, bucking and riding the orgasm. He gripped her ass and drove deeper as she cried out and fell apart under his touch.

Two movies, half a dozen chocolate chip cookies with mugs full of cold chocolate, and one other amazing round of sex later, Bree was asleep in Beau's arms, spooned into the bend of him. He was completely and satisfyingly spent. There was nowhere else he wanted to be.

He was happy.

As he began to drift into a sleepy haze, Beau thought about the promotion and taking McAllister's place on the management team. He wasn't willing to give happiness up for money anymore. For so long, it seemed like if he could just make something of himself at work, he could prove he was a man, *the* man for Bree. Someone who could provide and protect her. For all his ambition, he'd ended up alone.

One thing was for sure, if giving the promotion up meant getting Bree back, he'd do it in a heartbeat.

The staticky crackle of the intercom ripped through the quiet hum of the plane as the captain turned off the fasten seatbelt sign. Within moments, the flight attendants began to move around the cabin for a drink service, and Aubrey was thankful for the empty seat beside her.

She didn't have the energy to force a conversation out of thin air or to plaster on a happy face for a stranger's sake. It was bad enough she'd have to wear the mask all weekend for Matt's engagement party. She just needed the next few hours to herself to drift away, wake up in Chicago, and make it to her old room where she could fall apart in peace.

A giant tote bag plopped down on the seat beside Aubrey and she about jumped out of her skin.

"I'm sorry. I didn't mean to wake you," a busy gray-haired woman huffed without looking up. "I can't find my doggone sanitizer. The guy sitting next to me..." she whispered, bending her index finger before angling it near her nose to demonstrate his apparent nose-digging action.

Aubrey winced, wrinkled her nose, and gave the woman a twisty, disgusted smile as she sniffled. "Ew."

"Ugh. I know. Some people." The woman was still fishing her hand down to the bottom of the bag, presumably hunting for a travel-sized bottle buried underneath everything *and* the kitchen sink when she finally lifted her head to meet Aubrey's gaze.

She realized how she must look to the woman.

"Oh..." The woman's warm, brown eyes went wide as she bit her lip and pressed her hand to her chest, taking in Aubrey's tears. "Are you okay, sweetheart? I didn't mean to...I just... Can I get you anything?"

There it was. Everything Aubrey was feeling reflected back at her. The pity, the sadness, and the heartbreak was evident on her face. She swallowed the lump in her throat and shook her head as the lady gathered the tote into her arms.

When she walked away, Aubrey turned back to the tiny bubble window, unblinking, unseeing as the plane waded through a sea of fluffy, white clouds. Her blotchy cheeks and dark circles beneath her eyes were visible in her blurry reflection. The hollow ache in her heart and the emptiness were proof it was real.

For the second time in six months, she'd walked out on Beau.

More accurately, she'd slinked away while he slept.

Her heart slogged in her chest, struggling to beat, and her mouth quivered as she held back a sob. Something about this time felt final. Beau wouldn't call for weeks leaving adorably, desperate messages, telling her how much he loved and missed her with his "whole aching heart" and how seeing her freckles dancing across the bridge of her perky nose first thing in the morning kept him walking on sunshine throughout the day. No, he wouldn't send pink tulips or ask the few mutual friends they still shared to check in on her. He wouldn't do any of those things because on a single page of hotel paper, written in jagged script, she'd asked him not to.

More than ever, she knew she'd made the right decision. Before she boarded the flight, she'd received a call from Shane's girlfriend, *her* friend, Nadia, asking if Aubrey went back to Beau's room. When Aubrey asked how she knew about the hotel, Nadia told her she'd overheard the conversation between Beau and Shane. He'd decided to win Aubrey back if she showed up. But then right after that, Nadia mentioned Beau was up for another promotion.

Another rung on the corporate ladder.

Another mountain between them.

Aubrey huddled in the corner closer to the window and stifled a yawn. It seemed as good a time as any to shut her eyes and drift far away. Except, as soon as she did, she felt the shift in the cushion beneath her as someone sat beside her in the aisle seat.

Please don't try to talk to me.

Aubrey listened, wondering what the person was doing. She'd noticed the flight attendants were a few rows ahead of hers just a couple of minutes ago. The person was probably just moving out of the aisle to give them room to pass. Or, maybe it was the sanitizer woman again back to check on her.

She relaxed her shoulders and evened her breathing, careful not to let on that she was awake. But then, she heard the twist and click of the tray table being let down...in front of her. *Shit.* The person moved again and then she heard the sound of paper rustling. At the risk of being found out, she cracked her eyes open to tiny slits and peeked out.

On her tray was the ripped paper with her jagged script.

"You didn't wake me."

Beau.

Aubrey held her breath and inclined her head. Her brows drew together and then a tear fell free.

"Why are you doing this?" Beau asked. Even though she wasn't looking directly at him, she could see the way he squared his body to her, looking into her, reading her. She sensed the unchecked emotion in his tone. He was asking for more from her.

Words wouldn't pass Aubrey's lips, so she turned to meet his gaze, which was a mistake. Tears swam in his red eyes. He still looked completely disheveled with his sex-ravaged, bed-head hair, and that mouth… Lord, his mouth was simply irresistible and full. His lower lip sort of hung open, begging to be sucked and kissed until it was properly swollen and pink.

Another tear fell, blazing the curve of her cheek, pushing the other one down until it dropped. She watched as it seeped into her jeans, spreading into a depthless hole. She wanted to fall away into it.

"Beau." His name cracked on her tongue and a fresh wave of tears welled in her eyes and began streaming down her cheeks. "I can't."

With the pads of his fingers, he swiped her tears away, kissed her cheeks, then her eyes, and, finally, her lips. It was slow and gentle, steeped in need, just the way Aubrey liked it.

"I love you. I don't want to keep pretending I'm okay without you. I'm not. I want to be with you. I want us to be together." There was urgency in his tone, like if he didn't say it all at once he wouldn't be able to.

She didn't know where she found the words, but it was like the dam broke and the silence was over. Everything she'd been feeling for the past six months, and even before that, back from when he was working ten- to twelve-hour shifts, all came hurtling toward him.

"Nothing has changed. You haven't changed. We want different things, and I don't want to resent you, or have you resent me because of that. It's okay. What I said in the letter, it was all true. I have loved you since I was fifteen and I will always love you, but I can't allow myself to be second fiddle or just thank my lucky stars because you chose me at all. I'm a person, and I'm worth more. I'm more than just some puppy in a pound, who'll just be happy to see you when you get home."

Her voice was getting louder.

She looked around and lowered her volume but remained steadfast in what she had to say before she couldn't. "The way I see it, we shared a beautiful few hours together, and it was amazing. I would never take them back. It felt like an early Christmas gift to me." She laughed despite the gaping hole in her heart as she continued. "But, even when we were together, we weren't really together, Beau. Again, I'm going to ask you respect what I said in the letter. Let me deal with this my way. Give me space to heal."

A small part of her died the second the words crossed her tongue. Her insides rattled and it rocked her to her core. That it would all be fine eventually was the lie she kept telling herself. This wasn't what she wanted at all. If some mystery saint happened to be granting Christmas wishes, she'd ask for a happy, fulfilled Beau, wrapped in festive red and white polka dot paper with a giant bow on top. But that would never happen because nothing in his career ever fulfilled him. Nothing was enough.

"Go and be there for Grandma Hattie, and send her my wish for a speedy recovery. Really be there for her. Okay?"

"Please," he said.

"I'm serious. We can't keep doing this to ourselves," she replied firmly. *I can't keep pretending.*

Beau stared at her for a long while with round eyes and his square jaw hard-set. He brooded silently. She could see the wheels in his head turning, likely figuring how to spin a new ending, but soon enough, she saw the hope fading. He seemed to come to the same conclusion: what they shared was beautiful, but it was over.

It was never going to be enough for either of them.

Slowly, Beau leaned back against the seat and let his chin rest on his chest, before reaching his hand across the seat and twining their fingers. With a light squeeze, he pulled their hands to his mouth and kissed the back of hers.

His voice was thick with emotion and barely above a whisper. "I know you don't believe me, but it was only ever for you. All these years, I've been reaching and striving to be the man you deserve and that you would be proud to call yours—a man who could provide for you. I never wanted you to worry about anything, and I know money isn't important, but it can give you the freedom to choose what kind of life you want to live."

He cleared his throat. "You were never second to me. You're my first everything. You're my *reason* for everything."

Aubrey's mind drifted back to a night fourteen years ago beneath the pines and a sky blanketed with twinkling stars crowded around the moon. He'd kissed every inch of her body and promised to make her his first everything, and he was. He was the first and only man she'd given her body to, her first love, the first man she'd lived with who wasn't her father, and the first to completely and irrevocably break her heart.

Beau squeezed her hand again and the charms on her bracelet jingled loose from her sleeve.

"You're still wearing it?"

"Always," she whispered.

With his right hand, he fingered each of the fifteen silver charms. All were gifts from him, marking the important moments in their life together. There were the two teensy graduation caps on a ring together from their high school graduation. It was the beginning of their "us against the world" crusade. He'd said the world wasn't ready for a love like theirs.

About eight of them were from each of the states they'd visited together. And although it was technically an apartment, he'd given her a house charm at the beginning of their second year in college when they first moved out of the dorms, followed by a cute little wedding ring he promised to give her as soon as he could afford the real thing.

It was the last three that meant the most to Aubrey.

The charms were hearts in varying sizes and colors—a pink pavé diamond one, a red one painted with white dots, and a flat silver one with their initials engraved on the front. The last three years, he'd given her his heart and promised to give it to her every year after to remind her that she was its rightful owner and to take special care of it.

"I'm afraid I haven't done a great job, but in all fairness, you haven't taken such good care of mine, either." A laugh-cry sputtered from her lips. "I'm sorry. This is really hard."

A slow smile toyed at Beau's lips. "I know. Just… May I ask for one last favor?"

Aubrey bit her lip and tossed a smile back at him. "We don't have much time, and you don't have any peanuts or pretzels to bargain with for a fair trade."

He laughed, and the sound of his deep bass rumbling gave her a small piece of joy to hold onto.

Then his smile faded.

"I'm going to respect your wish and leave you alone." He cleared his throat again. "But…may I just be here with you like this for the rest of the flight? Please do this one little thing for me. I need it."

Without hesitation, she nodded and tightened her fingers around his. As much as Aubrey didn't want to admit it, she needed it, too. For an hour a half more, they sat in silence, absorbing the last of their great love.

The irony of it didn't escape her. In that very moment, she decided a love like theirs wasn't ready for the world.

MERRY CHRISTMAS BABY

"Thanks for that."

Beau stood in the aisle as the other passengers rushed to grab their luggage in the race to be the first off of the plane. He was stuck between some burly guy with a bag that was obviously too big to be a carry-on and a woman yelling into her phone that they'd just landed, and she'd be down to passenger pick-up shortly.

He glanced back at Aubrey who still hadn't moved. Her hand was still in the spot on the seat where he'd been holding it with all of his might only minutes before, and she was staring at him. Beau knew the way she felt, but for the life of him, he couldn't fathom how she could let them go so easily. She was all he ever knew and the only person he'd ever loved…would ever love.

"Happy holidays." He shook his head. "Or, rather, merry Christmas if I don't see you." He corrected himself.

"To you and Grandma Hattie, as well," Aubrey said. "Please send her my love and a wish for a speedy recovery."

"I will. She'll be happy to know you're doing well."

Up ahead, the line began to move, and people shifted and shoved forward. Although there were still people pulling their luggage down from the overhead bins, the anxious ones behind them were reeling and champing at the bit to get going. Even in the last rows, people stood and crowded the aisle.

His own bags were still up in business class. "All right, then. Looks like it's almost me. My stuff is up front."

"Yeah."

It was one word, but the breathless way she said it made Beau cling to it. He was on edge, praying there was more behind it. All he needed was one "but" or maybe a "see you soon." It would be enough. He would take anything he could.

Just then, the woman sitting behind them stood with her huge tote bag. Her eyes were watery, her skin pocked with blotchy pink spots, and she was shaking her head.

"Are you all right?" he asked her. "Can I do anything for you?"

Her lips pushed out as she swallowed and wiped away a tear. "There's got to be some kind of way!" she cried.

"Yes. Just tell me what you need. Is it water or tissue?" Beau asked. "Are you feeling ill? I can get the flight attendant for you just as soon as the line clears." He jammed his hands in his pockets searching for something—tissue or a piece of candy. Maybe she was diabetic and her blood sugar was low. His grandmother lived across the country, but old habits died hard, and he usually kept a butterscotch or peppermint hard candy with him at all times just in case.

Bree turned in her seat. Her eyes were just as forlorn. She looked as wrecked as he felt.

Maybe I shouldn't have come back here.

This wasn't what he wanted at all. Maybe he should have just listened and let her have her space.

The woman's dire expression caught the attention of other passengers and now everyone around was looking on, ready to jump into action, or to take videos to post. What a story. *I saved a woman before I deplaned.*

The woman's eyes flitted between Bree and Beau and she was

still shaking her head. "You love each other. There has to be a way for you to be together," she announced to the cabin.

The swarm of eyes landed on Beau and Bree.

The woman had apparently been listening the whole time. All around, everyone seemed to be dialed into the action. The watery red eyes and the forlorn expressions spread like contagion. Another woman with bright blue hair pressed her hand to her chest, and one of the flight attendants who'd passed by them several times placed one hand on her hip and the other over her mouth.

When the camera phones came out, Beau whipped his gaze back to Bree. He barely moved his lips as he swallowed and said the words aloud.

"I'll love her until the day I die, but she doesn't want me."

An audible gasp pierced the silence and it was too much to take. The weight of it crashed down on his shoulders and his heart plummeted. He didn't want to be another episode on some YouTube "crazy things you see on a plane" channel.

"Excuse me. I've got to go." He pardoned himself as he weaved through the people, leaving Bree behind.

By the time Beau made it off the plane and into the gate area, he was breathless and completely losing his shit. He set his bags down and let the shallow breaths come until they evened out.

The woman was right. There was something inherently wrong about real love not working out. It seemed like as hard as it was to find it in a world full of billions of people, he should hold onto it as tightly as he could and never let go, at least not willingly.

Beau cracked his neck and pulled his shoulders back.

It wasn't right.

He couldn't just accept it. He had to find Bree and beg.

*A*ubrey waited for the last of the people to exit the plane. When there was no one else around beyond the flight attendants tidying up, she finally stood, pulled her bag from the overhead bin, and dragged it down the aisle. It was so heavy, it felt more like it was dragging her.

The tweeters and posters got their show. They got something to talk about, and she'd seen her pain reflected back at her.

Seeing the tears in Beau's eyes and the way he rushed off, it tore her heartstrings loose and left her floating outside of her body. Had she really just let him walk away? Was this how she wanted it to end?

No.

She walked a little faster. Maybe she could still catch up to him.

"Safe travels," the willowy flight attendant from earlier said as Aubrey passed the row she cleaned. She had sympathetic round eyes and unmistakable pity beneath spidery lashes. There was no *have a nice day* or *hope the rest of your day goes better* behind her tight smile.

No sense in sugar-coating, Aubrey thought. It was obvious, she wouldn't have a nice day and it wouldn't get any better. *Where else is there to go from here? I just let the love of my life walk away and did nothing to stop him.*

Aubrey bit back the thick emotions clogged in her throat. "Thanks. You too." Her voice sounded as shaky and uneven as she felt. All she wanted to do was go back home, crawl into bed, eat a giant bag of Flamin' Hot Cheetos, and sleep for as long as it took to forget everything that happened in the past twenty-four hours.

Holidays be damned.

As soon as she made it off the plane and down to baggage claim, it became glaringly obvious forgetting wasn't an option.

Note to self: Never ask where to go from here. Down is a long, long way.

She stopped in her tracks then stumbled back a couple of steps. Her eyes widened and her heart plummeted. She couldn't breathe as she looked right, then left, then right again in a mental tug-of-war.

This seriously can't be happening.

There was Beau, looking apologetic and adorably disheveled with his big, upturned glossy gray eyes and flushed cheeks. He hadn't left. All of his bags were at his feet, and his hands were jammed into his pockets.

Beau shrugged, and the corner of his mouth hitched up in a sexy half-smile.

He was staring right at her like at any moment he might run to her and say everything she'd been dying to hear all these months. They were at this deep-ditch fork in the road, and, finally, he was ready to make his move.

Aubrey opened her mouth then promptly closed it again.

Shit.

She tightened her grip on the suitcase handle and flashed a small smile before stealing her gaze away and forcing it to the left. *Dammit! Not now, Mom.*

Any other time, Ellen Green couldn't be bothered to tear herself away from whatever dinner party or crafts club she packed her schedule with, but today of all days, she was in the airport. There she was, cheerier than ever, in a loud, yet tastefully crocheted, Christmas sweater set that probably cost an arm and two legs.

Aubrey tossed a glance back over to Beau, her brows pinched together in longing. It was like she'd finally decided on a show to binge-watch then found out the next season was cancelled—eternal cliffhanger. There was no way she was going to go through the motions with Beau now and feed Mom's ammo arsenal to rag on her life decisions later.

"Give me just…" she trailed off, holding up a finger to Beau as she strode toward her mother.

"There you are. We were beginning to think you missed another flight," Mom gushed in her velvety velour voice. Aubrey was just about to make some elaborate excuse that would get her out of rehashing the gambit of events from the last hours of her hell day when a single word snagged her attention.

It was like a teensy *Ping!*

We.

What in the actual f—?

How had she missed him? He was unmissable. Next to Mom, blending in like a rainbow toe sock in a row of silk stockings, was Trey Stone. Not only was he right there in plain sight, her mom was holding his hand.

"I...I..." The words literally wouldn't pass her tongue, but her mind was still functioning on all cylinders, and everything started to make sense.

Aubrey's eyes drifted to her mom's smarmy smile. She was even wearing extra red lipstick *and* the fancy pearls she usually wore to impress Dad's work friends.

Oh, yeah. She leaned forward slightly and sniffed. Sweet, tangy Miss Dior Cherie.

Well, no wonder. This is a freaking setup.

Her mouth slowly fell open and she squinted her eyes and shook her head.

Her mom was positively buoyant with her dainty fingers draped around Trey's massive ones. She was guilty...and shady. He was the reason she'd been nagging Aubrey to hurry home. This wasn't just another random dude her mother was trying to fix her up with. This was Trey Stone—the big-time soccer star Aubrey crushed hard on during her freshmen and sophomore years of high school before Beau transferred from Northern Illinois. He'd been disgustingly filthy rich and a grade-A douchebag with an ego that could barely be contained within the walls of the airport.

But that was ten years ago.

Time had a way of magnifying a person's outlook on life. Here she couldn't find an hour in the day to submit the single most important article of her career. Meanwhile, Trey's Magic 8-Ball always came back with, "outlook good."

To go along with his towering height and youthful Fresh Prince quirky good looks, he'd become a local news anchor and an Instagram influencer with about two million followers and fake friends to inflate his ego. Aubrey was not one of them. She still hadn't quite gotten around to following him back even though she might have scanned his page once or twice when she was drunk and nursing a bruised ego.

Twice.

Okay, three times, but that was neither here nor there.

To add insult to injury, now he was apparently moonlighting as an escort for a thirty-year-old who couldn't get a date to her brother's engagement party.

Seriously, Mom? Why?

She shook her head again and trained a deep gaze on Mom. "What exactly are you trying to do here?" Then she flashed Trey a quick smile. "Hey. Let me guess, you're the surprise?"

He nodded and held up his hands, palms out.

As suspected, her mom was definitely the culprit, which by her cheery disposition, she seemed completely okay with. There was no telling what that woman came up with to get him to agree to be Aubrey's date. You don't blame the fly when he gets stuck in the spider's web.

Aubrey sighed and hugged Trey in spite of her mother.

Of course, that's when Beau sauntered up.

"This guy? Really?" He looked at Aubrey like he didn't even know her...like she was a disappointment. "It figures."

Her heartbeat pounded in her ears, and she wanted to reach for him and pull him into a corner to finally hash this thing between them out, but she held back. Beau's tone was filled with disdain and accusation. The way he kept shaking his head made her want to press pause and think for a second, but it was too late. It was all happening too fast.

"Please, just give me a second," she pleaded with Beau.

In classic mom form, her mother couldn't resist adding her two cents. "Now, this is neither the time nor the place for something like this. We have a whole house full of family and friends waiting for us back at the house, and Trey was nice enough to drive, so let's not be rude. Plus…" Aubrey cringed, dreading what her mom would say next since Beau was basically on her shit list after simultaneously crushing Aubrey's heart and her dreams of planning another wedding. "I believe Beau had his chance, and it did not fare well for you, as I recall."

Suckerpunch to the gut.

"Mom, stop." Aubrey squeezed her eyes shut and massaged her fingers over her temples. "I need some time to talk to Beau. Please don't make a big deal."

Beau's mouth twisted into a wry smile like this whole situation was typical—exactly what he'd expected from her mother. He set his jaw and even with his mouth closed, she could tell his teeth were clenched and biting back his emotion. A mixture of anger, betrayal, and hurt flared in his eyes, but he shook his head and scrubbed his hands over his face as if he was trying to wipe it all away.

"It's cool. I don't want to cause a scene or anything. I'm good." He stepped backward, nodding as his lip curved into a smirk. Then he eyed Trey. "I'll just…leave you to your surprise."

Then, he faded into the crowd.

I'LL BE HOME FOR CHRISTMAS

By the time Beau made it to the hospital, he needed to see his grandmother in the worst way. His mind was all over the place, and he felt like if he could just talk to her, she could help him figure out how he and Bree had let themselves get lost in the shuffle.

He used to be so sure everything would work out, and they'd end up back together eventually, but now, he wasn't so certain.

Trey fucking Stone.

The elevator door opened on the seventh floor and Beau weaved through the halls until he arrived at his grandmother's hospital room. He didn't enter immediately. For a few seconds, he scrubbed his hand over his face and blew out a calming breath in an effort to compose himself before seeing her.

When he was ready, he twisted his lips into a smile and walked in. "Hey. There she is!"

"Hi," she whispered, sounding breathy and drained.

Hattie Redgrave was a woman of many faces. Most of the time, she wore a peaceful grin etched between her hard-earned laugh lines. If you got her hot enough to boil her blood, she kept a hard-core, no-nonsense face tucked away for just that occasion. Beau had been lucky enough to be raised by her, so he knew there was an Oscar-worthy, sullen, puckered lip, puppy dog-eyed face she saved for the times she really wanted something.

The corners of Beau's mouth hitched up in a knowing smile. "And the Academy Award goes to..." He paused for dramatic effect before blowing hot air like an audience roar. "The crowd is going wild! It's Hattie Redgrave."

He planted a giant, wet smooch on her cheek and gathered her into a hug, holding her while he stared deeply into her warm, brown eyes.

"Aw shucks. I never could fool you."

"I know, you big faker. Is any of this even real? They're going to pull the curtain any minute, and I'll know you're paying a bunch of actors to dress up like doctors and nurses." He guffawed, plopping down on the hard chair beside the bed.

The happy face was back, and her smooth, sagging skin twisted into an ear-to-ear smile.

"See, this is why I love you. Even when you're down for a few minutes you get right back up again." Beau tugged the blanket and tucked it tighter underneath her feet. "You're not off the hook completely, though."

For the next half hour, Beau chastised his grandmother about eating properly and making sure her blood sugar didn't get too low. When the nurse, a young guy wearing glasses and Iron Man scrubs, came to check on his grandma, Beau took the opportunity to drill him then eventually recruit him to double-team her about the seriousness of her disease.

After she'd eaten, they talked about her church friends and Mr. Freckles, her cat, who was staying with her neighbor while she was in the hospital. Eventually, the conversation dried up.

"Remember after Mom died, how you used to get clothing donations from the church?" Beau slouched down into the chair and let his head rest on the back.

"Mmm hmm," she replied.

He stretched his legs out in front of him and stared absently at the television. "I got this blue and green sweater from one of the bags. It was nice and warm with no tears or snags, and it looked like it was practically new, so I wore it to school the next day."

"Yeah."

"Anyway, it turned out it used to belong to Trey Stone, who basically hated me. Remember him?"

She sucked her teeth and pursed her lips. "I sure do. That's the boy you had that scuffle with. He got you suspended."

"Uh, huh. He went around school announcing to everyone that I was trash-digger and I was homeless, so I punched him, and he called me a bastard. He said Mom and Dad would rather kill themselves than be parents to me." Beau hadn't thought about that sweater in years, but somehow, he could feel its soft fabric brush over his skin like it was yesterday.

"Anyway, after that, I sort of set my mind to making something of myself. I never wanted to let someone like Trey get to me like that again." He sighed and peeked over at Grandma as she lowered the volume on the television.

"You know, you're not the only one who knows how to read faces," she said.

"Yeah? What's mine telling you?"

They were both still staring at some gameshow on the television, but her intuition was what Beau was counting on.

"Where'd you see her?"

He turned and studied her for a moment. The grin was there but her brows were knitted together.

"She was on my flight." Beau paused, pulled his bottom lip between his teeth, and rubbed the pad of his finger over his top lip as he decided how much to say. "We spent some time together, but…it's over. She doesn't want to work it out."

The inflection in his voice rose up on the last sentence and seemed to snag his grandma's attention. She turned to face him. "Is that so?"

"Yes."

"A long time ago, I was a young woman in love with your grandfather, and when he was too stupid to see what he had right in front of him, I made him work for it. When he was too busy trying to make something of himself, I left. I told him it was over just to let him feel what it was like to lose me because sometimes that's what it takes. You men are so damned thick-headed."

Beau's grandparents were married for fifty-one years before his grandfather passed away, and he'd never known anything about this part of the story. He'd placed them up on a pedestal as the great love to model his and Bree's relationship after, but, somehow, he'd missed the point that they were real people with flaws and fragile hearts who'd chosen each other.

"Hattie Redgrave. I can't believe you. Here I thought you were this sweet little innocent old lady and now I find our you're a gambling, ultimatum-giver. You tricked Grandpa."

"No. I just helped him get out of his own way."

"Same thing."

"Well, how else was I going to get him to see that we were destined to end up together?"

She might have been his grandmother, but underneath all the mothering and sage advice, she was still a woman. Beau shook his head, amazed at the depths of the crazy, funny, genius…woman.

His heart was pounding against his chest, and suddenly his skin pulsed and he had butterflies. He was feeling something like hope.

"So what should I do?" He raked his hands over his head with a big cheesy smile.

It's not over.

"Well that depends on what you're willing to do and how much you love her."

"Anything." He was breathless.

Grandma slid her soft hand over his and squeezed. "Are you

about done making something of yourself, or are you still running in place and getting nowhere?"

Maybe Shane's advice wasn't so bad.

Beau knew exactly what his grandma meant. He couldn't take the position even if Davenport hand-picked him. All this time, he trying to climb to the top when he was already there. He was always at his highest with Bree next to him.

"I have to see her."

"There he is ladies and gentleman," Grandma mocked him as she leaned over to the nightstand and pulled out a crisp, red envelope with gold calligraphy and passed it to Beau. "You know Ellen Green and I have been friends for a long time. She may or may not have stopped by to check on me yesterday."

He was still smiling as he pulled out the invitation to Matthew Green's engagement party. It seemed he had a party to crash—and a long overdue phone call to make.

*T*he drive home from the airport was a special kind of hell.

Not only did Trey drive an overcompensating, flashy sports car, but it was a stuffy, hot coupe. It was certainly expensive, but still a coupe. So, while he drove, and Aubrey sat shotgun sweating her ass off and battling a headache from his woodsy cologne, behind them, her mom's butt straddled the line between the incredibly tight two backseats. It was even more awesome when she leaned forward between the two front seats to "feel like part of the conversation."

In actuality, the only time she stopped commandeering the one-way direction of the conversation was to sing—loudly and off-key—along to Justin Bieber's *Mistletoe*.

"Wait until you see the tree this year," she purred as Trey merged onto the Dan Ryan Expressway. "I've got this rustic-chic, red and black buffalo check theme going, and it's..." In the rearview mirror, Aubrey saw her mom's flailing "mind-blown" gesture. "Ooh. You just have to see it. I got the idea on one of those home decorating shows with that couple..."

Aubrey and Trey barely got a word in edgewise. Her mom ensured every lull in the conversation was conveniently filled. Initially, she talked about the upcoming Christmas festivities through the weekend and into next week. From there, she took a tangent into her famous "favorite things," Oprah-esque gift give-away, then to the minute-to-win-it games she was planning—the tissue box twerk was Aubrey's personal favorite.

As expected, lest she show any sign of being a humanoid who cared about her daughter's well-being, noticeably absent in her spiel was any mention of Beau and the airport dramatics.

Aubrey let that lion lay. It seemed counterproductive to revisit the wound when it was still so fresh.

She stared out the window at the blur of cars smearing by in a neon rainbow, thankful for the distraction. If she didn't think about Beau, she could almost ignore the fact she didn't know exactly what she was waiting on before she would take him back. Seeing him waiting for her as she got off the plane, vulnerable, it was important. It was enough to get her to pay attention. Yes, he was still climbing the ladder, but his priorities were shifting.

Maybe he'd changed.

People can change, can't they?

She couldn't quite put her finger on it, but it was one of those, "I'll know it when I see it," type of feelings. Gambling with her heart was a little risky, but she had to go with her gut, especially if she didn't want to feel like she'd settled.

"Tourettes."

The word snagged Aubrey's attention as she caught the tail end of what Mom said. She twisted in her seat to meet her mother's wild brown eyes.

"What?"

"The cookie is on your forehead, and you have to move your head or your brows to work it down to your mouth," Mom explained, and Aubrey still had no clue what she was saying.

She lowered her chin and felt the crease between her brows deepen. "What are you talking about?"

Beside her, Aubrey noticed Trey's shoulders bouncing as he bit back a grin while her mother proceeded to fill her in on what she'd missed while she was stuck in her own head. Her mom was going over the instructions for another minute-to-win-it game where a cookie is placed on the player's forehead, and without using hands, the goal is to get the cookie into his or her mouth, which made the players look crazy "like they've got facial tics or Tourette syndrome."

"Oh." Aubrey sighed. Leave it to her mother to make light of Tourette syndrome.

"Actually, the games sound pretty hilarious." Trey laughed and looked past Aubrey to change lanes. She noticed something in his eyes. They were warm and kind—nothing like the pair that belonged to the jerk she remembered.

Could *he* have changed?

It seemed so drastic, that he'd make a full one-eighty personality change.

Aubrey definitely wasn't the same person she was ten plus years ago. She was just about to spiral down the memory rabbit hole, but then he caught her looking.

Her lips parted, even though she didn't know what to say. She wasn't attracted to him, but she wanted to know who this new Trey was. She wanted to ask something profound or personal. What was the catalyst to his change? Of course, that's when her mom started singing again and the moment seemed lost.

Aubrey and Trey exchanged a glance that was amused on his part and apologetic on hers. She shrugged and mouthed "sorry." She was mortified that he was being subjected to her mother's machinations, but he seemed genuinely nonplussed. Aubrey couldn't help but to give him back one of the billion cool points she'd taken from him all those years ago.

They hadn't shared more than ten words between them with Motormouth Maybelle in the car, but Aubrey had a hunch he wasn't the same guy from high school. She was sad that he wouldn't have a fighting chance to prove how much he'd changed.

When he slowed to a stop at a red light, she flashed him a genuine smile, making a note to follow him back on Instagram and to take a little time at the cocktail party to catch up. Apparently, people were changing all around her.

After circling the block twice, Trey found a parking space three houses down from her parent's. In true Ellen Green fashion, she'd invited everyone they knew to the engagement party, and by the number of random cars in the cul-de-sac, at least ninety percent of them showed up early.

"This should be fun," Aubrey flashed Trey an animated smile and sighed. She watched as her breath danced and dissolved in the air.

Her mom hugged Trey and urged Aubrey to hurry and get cleaned up for cocktail hour before she scurried off to tend to her guests, leaving the two of them outside in the brisk cold.

A shiver coursed through her, and she jammed her hands into her coat pockets, feeling the cool surface of her phone. God, she wanted to call Beau so badly, but what was she going to say? Plus, he still thought there was something going on between her and Trey.

"Are you ready to go inside?" Trey held his arms close to his to body and he appeared to clench his teeth to keep them from chattering. "I'm freezing."

She didn't know why she was hesitating, but she couldn't bring herself to move her feet. "Can I ask you something?"

"Quickly."

Aubrey laughed. "Okay. You saw Beau, right?"

He nodded and raised his brows, urging her to get to the point before they both turned to into popsicles.

"I know this is kind of weird to ask you, but I get the sense that you're completely different from the person you were back in high school. You seem more relaxed and kind-hearted. That's just a vibe I'm getting."

Trey laughed. "I know. I was such a little shit back then, but thanks for noticing the improvement. I'm kind of working on being a better human."

"I get that," Aubrey said. "My thought process is that if you could change, maybe Beau could, too. He wasn't an asshole or anything. Just the opposite. He was pretty much everything I ever wanted in a man, but I don't feel like I'll ever be enough for him." She was rambling, and she knew it. She paused for a brief second, to get a hold of herself, but it was pointless. "He just works himself to the bone like he's got something to prove to people, and it doesn't leave much time for anything else. *Anyone else*, I should say."

"So, you love him?" Trey watched her carefully. She knew he was scrutinizing her for any sign of hesitation when she answered.

Aubrey didn't have to think about it twice.

"Yes. I've always loved him. He's pretty much it for me, but I need him to feel the same way and to be willing to fight for us." The second the words passed her lips Aubrey knew it was what she'd been waiting for. Before she would take him back, she needed to know he wouldn't give up. It was why seeing him waiting for her in the airport earlier had rattled her insides loose. She didn't want to tell him what she needed. He had to figure it out on his own.

She wanted Beau to know she was the only woman for him and to fight for and choose her.

"Just to play devil's advocate here, what if he doesn't fight for you?" Trey asked. "Would you write him off and let the relationship go?"

In the back of her mind, Aubrey had never considered that possibility. They were always going to find their way back to each other. Six months was longer than she figured he would need, but she never thought he wouldn't fight for her at all.

Her mind raced and her heartbeat sped up. Inside her pocket, she found the tiny hole and poked her finger inside before closing her eyes.

What if I've lost him?

The whole world closed in on her and she was back in the social worker's small, dingy white car driving away. There had been a small hole in the seat fabric that looked like it came from a cigarette burn. It wasn't immediately noticeable, but she'd been in that backseat so many times, it became a strange source of comfort—something she could count on. She'd stick her finger inside and hold on to the sound of the music and the hum of the old car to block out the words she'd heard too many times.

"They didn't choose to keep you."

Each time she'd left a family, a little more of her hope stayed behind. After so long, the tears had dried up and her heart had almost completely hardened when Ellen and Maxwell Green appeared in her life with a young son and a dream of having the daughter Ellen's body couldn't give them. They chose her, fought for her, and softened her heart again.

Her heart still had a tiny hole in it, but every day with her new family, every time her articles were selected by magazines, and falling in love with Beau helped her to become whole.

Tears spilled from her eyes, hot against her cold skin, and she looked up to meet Trey's steady gaze.

"If he doesn't fight for me, well, I guess I'll have to show him we're worth fighting for." Aubrey swiped a tear from her cheek and smiled up at Trey, who shrugged and tossed her an *I-guess-you-got-your-answer* look. She went in for a full-body bear hug, burying her face into his chest. "Who knew you were going to grow up to be so useful, and easy to talk to, and…non-douchey."

They both broke out in laughter.

"All right, lightweight champ, any chance we can go inside where I won't freeze my balls off before you start throwing jabs?" Trey asked.

"And there he is." She shook her head in mock annoyance. "I cannot believe you said 'balls.' See, I knew you were hiding in there somewhere. Welcome back."

In that moment, she didn't know if change was overrated or not, but it was definitely possible.

As they walked the few feet to the house, Aubrey felt lighter and bounced with the extra spring in her step. The Green Mix and Mingle Bell Rock cocktail party was in an hour. The way she was feeling, she could bang out her article, shower, do a few dozen burpees, and still have time to spare. Once she had her mind set and the gloves on, she was unstoppable.

SANTA CLAUS IS COMING
TO TOWN

*T*hat night, Beau shifted from foot to foot and adjusted the lapels of his jacket against the evening chill as he inhaled a sharp breath and blew it out slowly. He pressed the doorbell and stood up taller. The party was already in full force. By the number of cars parked out front and the volume level blaring through the door, the toasts wouldn't be far off.

This is a bad idea.

Back at the hospital with Grandma pumping him up and adrenaline coursing through his veins, crashing Matt's party seemed like the thing to do. He'd already called Davenport to let him know he was going to pass on the position, so he was ready to prove himself to Bree. Now, standing outside the door with a half-assed plan to win her back and a cheap bottle of gas station champagne, Beau realized he hadn't completely thought this through.

There were too many unknown variables in play. He had no guarantees this would work. Bree might not be happy to see him, or she might *want* someone like Trey Stone, but Beau couldn't go off mights and maybes. If the last six months without Bree were any indication of his future, he really had no choice. He couldn't live with the regret of "what if."

"Come on. Answer."

He scrubbed his free hand over his face and pushed his shoulders back just as the door swung open.

"What are you doing here?"

Beau used to tease Matt Green about being a pretty boy. He looked like some guy you'd see on *The Bachelor*. He was clean-shaven with a baby face, side-swept dark hair, a cleft chin, and lineman broad shoulders. Tonight, he was even dressed for television, minus the rose. The expression on his face as he wedged himself in the doorframe was all business, though.

"Hey." Beau paused and scratched the bridge of his nose before lowering his chin. When he looked back up again, he realized there was no turning back. *Now or never.* He shrugged. "I fucked up."

For a brief moment, Matt seemed to eye him with guarded interest. His mouth was a hard line and he didn't say a word, which Beau assumed was meant to shake him up. It worked because Matt was only ever quiet when he was surprised or pissed. Beau was hoping his party-crash fell in the former category.

Wounded indignation swelled inside Beau, and he lifted his chin and bared his throat, but then he saw it. A glint of amusement in Matt's eyes.

"Well, no shit, Sherlock. The whole internet knows that. You guys have gone viral. Your little outburst ended up on Plane Confessions." A half grin tugged at the corner of Matt's mouth. "It's about time you got your shit together."

A wave of relief washed over Beau. He and Matt had been tight, but the second things were over with Bree, all the niceties were over. Seeing Matt now, playing the protective brother, made Beau realize how much he missed his friend.

They went in for a one-handed hug and patted each other on the back.

"Still my favorite pretty boy," Beau teased.

"I heard about all your drama at the airport...still a day late and a dollar short." Matt stepped back and shook his head. "So, you know she's here with Trey..."

Beau straightened his tie, smoothed the lapels of his jacket, and patted his pants pocket. "That's where you come in."

"Whoa, whoa, whoa. This my celebration night. Why couldn't you just show up on Christmas like every other sappy dude out there?"

"Because this can't wait." The words rushed out of Beau's mouth louder than he'd intended before he could stop them.

Matt held his palms up and peeked over his shoulder. "Okay. Relax. Trey is cool, but I don't want him as a brother. What's the plan?"

They slipped into the laundry room to hash out all the details, and no one appeared to be the wiser. Matt went back to the party, and Beau stayed in the laundry room to wait for his cue. Only when the door clicked shut behind Matt did he feel his body tense. His chest rose and fell with rapid breaths and his heart plummeted. He found himself imagining a future without Bree and a familiar tide of panic left him unbalanced.

Beau inhaled the scent of fabric softener and powder detergent, and a wave of nostalgia shook him to the core. He leaned against the dryer and for the first time in the longest time, he allowed himself to think about his mother. The last time he saw her, he was eight. Her suitcases were by the door and she was all bundled up in a puffy coat with the fur lining the hood. She was petite, so its mass swallowed her up. All he could see were her dainty hands and a glimpse of her face. Her light brown hair and dark brows framed bright, seafoam green eyes that were fringed with long lashes. Her smile was strained around the edges.

It was snowing outside, and they'd spent the morning making snow angels in the yard and drinking hot chocolate as an early Christmas celebration. She was leaving him with his grandmother for a year while she worked in the field with Bridging Borders. When she hugged him, she still smelled of pancakes and fresh laundry.

He could still feel the cold coming off her hands beneath the cotton of his shirt as she met his gaze.

There was a rasp to her voice as she eyed him with a wistful glance. "This is temporary. Two months is nothing. When I come back, we're going to get our own place and you'll get that Spiderman bedroom you want with webs in the corners, and a giant decal for your wall. We'll make it our own. It'll be you and me. Two peas in a pod. I love you so much."

It wasn't temporary.

She died of pneumonia before she could return, and he never told anyone about their dream. They never got to be two peas in a pod, or have their own place, and he never got his own bedroom.

The door opened with a whoosh. A cinnamon and pine aroma flooded his senses and he blinked out of his trance. From the other room, he could hear the sound of silverware clinking against glasses and Matt bringing the room to order.

Of all the people Beau could think of, he didn't expect to see Ellen Green holding the door handle and smiling at him.

"Don't look shocked." Her chin was held high, and she looked at him over the bridge of her nose. "You're not the only one who took a while to come around to their senses. When I saw my daughter at the airport, the sadness in her eyes, I knew you two belonged together. And then Matt showed me the video on the YouTube." She beamed and her eyes glistened.

Regret flared in Beau's gut as he found his footing and stood up taller. He didn't have any say in losing his mother, but he definitely wasn't going to give up on Bree. Deep down, he still wanted the two peas in a pod and their own place. He wanted the dream and the family.

Whether she was a hugger or not, he pulled Ellen in for a tight embrace and kissed her cheek before following her to the dining room. He hung back a few steps in the hall, but he could see the head of the table. Immediately, he spotted Bree. Her quiet beauty hit Beau like a wall. He was boneless, and emotion clogged in his throat.

It was about time he got out of his own way.

*E*ggnog was one of Aubrey's favorite drinks in in the whole world. Add in a few fingers of Dad's top-shelf bourbon, and...*wow!* Talk about packing a punch. She was closer to tipping over than tipsy, and the combination of her wily emotions over her big brother getting engaged and Trey's sarcastic commentary about the party guests left her stifling giggles and swiping at happy tears.

Laughter was the good stuff. So much better than thinking about how she'd royally fucked up with Beau, or how she'd submitted a totally amateur article, which Gena Detrich was probably using as kindling for her fireplace.

A bout of whistles and cheers erupted as Matt let another F-bomb slip.

Aubrey smiled and shrugged off her worries, adjusting in her chair to give her brother her full attention. She was sitting at the head of the table with her family as Matt made his toast. He'd been talking for a while and ticking off Mom's checklist to specifically respond to what the father of the bride-to-be said in his speech. It was something cliché and completely fitting about hunting and early birds. He'd also made sure to acknowledge that they were paying for Matt's and Sabrina's snazzy wedding next year, which, by the way her bourgeois mother was talking, would be an appropriately expensive event.

Bree was on her third eggnog when Matt got around to

thanking the friends that would make up their wedding party. His best friend, Eric, appeared to be less enthralled by his speech and laser-focused on the perky cleavage of Sabrina's younger sister. Matt finally wrapped up by thanking everyone else who'd come from the far ends of the earth to be there during the holiday weekend and toasting Sabrina.

That's when Aubrey's third eggnog tapped her bladder.

Psst...want to go shake the dew off the lily?

She beamed at her brother with a tight, clenched smile as she crossed her legs and squeezed. For extra security, she crossed her feet at the ankles and tried not to squirm.

Trey, who had turned out to be better than average company, was sitting next to her, and apparently as observant as he was sarcastic. He leaned in close to her ear and whispered, "Someone has to go tinkle."

"Shut up," she hissed.

He managed a closed-mouth giggle before sitting up ramrod straight. Since everyone was focused on her brother's speech, Trey was able to throw shade through his teeth. "It would be rude and poor etiquette to excuse yourself during your brother's heart-felt speech."

With her elbow, she jabbed him in the rib and covered her laugh with her hand.

Unfortunately, it seemed Matt still had a little more to say. "Okay, look guys, I thought I could hold out longer, but Sabrina can be very persuasive." Laughter erupted over the table and in the hall, and Aubrey nearly lost it. She squeezed her thighs tighter and bit down on her tongue in an effort to stifle the giggles bubbling up inside her.

"Really, I'm just as surprised as you are to be standing here announcing my engagement. The way I see it, it's no secret every woman has an idea of her dream wedding. My own sister even has a wedding scrapbook. Actually, it's a ten-volume opus of how the whole wedding is going to play out."

That did it. *Shit. I think a drop escaped.*

She adjusted herself in the chair and began to wiggle her legs.

"I'm for real," Matt continued. "There are even footnotes. Mom, I think we need to have her checked out."

"Don't do it," Trey whispered.

Aubrey started counting backward from one hundred, trying unsuccessfully to even her breathing. How did this speech become about her all of the sudden? Now everyone was looking at her amusedly. Lord have mercy, she wished she was wearing her granny panties instead of a piece of thread thong to avoid lines in her fitted dress.

"We guys never talk about the fact that we also want to get married to our dream woman someday. Granted, we imagine it happening way, way, way down the road, but we want a dream wedding, too."

Fuck. Come on Matt. Do me a solid and end this speech, and I will owe you big.

She cleared her throat, hoping to get his attention, but his eyes were trained on Sabrina.

"Sabrina…" He stopped for a moment and Aubrey knew he was finished with the jokes. "I don't think I knew what living was until I found you. I was just existing and going wherever the wind blew me. I was floating in the darkness, and you appeared—a crazy, wild, vibrant firefly. I was just drawn to you, and every day just got better and better. I love your mind, body, and soul. No matter what color you dye your hair, whether you wear makeup or not, if you decide you want more tattoos… I'm so in love with every inch of you, and I can't wait to spend the rest of my life with you."

Matt bent down to kiss Sabrina and the glass clinking started up again. He whispered something in her ear, and she nodded with an ear-to-ear grin. Then, he called for the room's attention again.

Are you kidding me?

"I'm going to ask you to raise your glasses for me just one more time. This is to my sister Bree and *her* happy ending."

Don't do this right now. At least let me pee first.

Aubrey felt the heat crawl up her neck and settle in her cheeks as she peeked over at Trey. That's when she caught sight of Beau walking into the room and the urgency to pee vanished, replaced by a knocking in her chest. She sat up straight, watching him move toward the head of the table.

She couldn't breathe, and every emotion in the world went through her body. She was anxious, happy, angry, annoyed, jealous, and numb all at once.

How? She turned to Trey. "Did you know about this?"

"No." He shrugged.

He seemed to be telling the truth, so she searched the room for her mother, and there it was on her face. *Guilty.*

Aubrey pressed her hand to her heart and she bit back the emotion in her throat as she watched Beau at the head of the table with Matt. His eyes were as wet as hers. The emotion of the evening took them both over.

Someone passed Beau a champagne flute. He took a moment to thank everyone for giving him a few minutes of their time, then he looked at her.

"I've also prepared a few words..." He looked anxious and adorable. "I'm nervous, so just bear with me for a second." Again, laughter erupted before it died down as he swallowed back his nerves. "You see, I've only ever loved one woman."

Aubrey pressed her fingers to her lips and blinked back the tears.

"Believe it or not, she's here tonight with someone else." At this, Aubrey released a laugh-cry and Trey very dramatically scooted a foot away from her with his palms raised in a display of his innocence. The crowd played its part with a mixture of laughs and boos.

"We met when we were fifteen, and I have no clue what she

saw in me, but I felt like the luckiest bastard alive. Sorry, Mrs. Green." He grinned as her mom cocked her head and flashed him a reprimanding glare. Her smile soon returned. "Somewhere along the way, I got so busy trying to prove I was good enough for her, I lost sight of the fact that I already had her.

"Matt used to tell me that I'm always a day late and a dollar short to everything. It took me exactly six months and five days to understand that losing Bree would be the worst mistake of my life, so I'm here tonight with you fine folks to make sure that doesn't happen." Beau fished his hand in his pocket and pulled out a small green box with a red bow. "Aubrey Green, I promised to give you my heart every year and this year is no different."

As he lifted the top, she expected to see a Christmas heart charm, but there was no way she could have prepared herself for the heart-shaped diamond ring nestled in the velvet. When she'd left, she'd given the ring back, but Beau held onto it, and had the diamonds reset.

"Mr. and Mrs. Green, if you'll give us your blessing again, and Matt, if you don't mind sharing your night with us, I'd love to marry Bree and spend the rest of my life proving to her she's the only person I'll ever choose."

He walked around the table until he was standing right in front of Aubrey and lowered himself onto one knee.

"Bree, I love you. Please give me this chance. Marry me?"

The raw emotion in his voice hit her right in the heart. She couldn't stop the tears from falling, but she was smiling as she covered his lips with hers and nodded. The kiss was urgent and steeped with need. He released a low growl and she could feel its deep timbre low in her belly. "Yes," she said as she kissed him. "I love you, too."

He brushed the pads of his thumbs over the curves of her cheeks, pulling her closer still. His eyes snapped open, hunger darkening his smoky gray eyes, and her heart tripped around in her chest. How had she thought she could ever be without him? A slow and sexy grin grew on his beautiful face, and her blush deepened.

She sucked in a breath, electricity coursing through her veins. "I've missed you."

"I've missed *you*," he rasped.

"No matter what we face from here on out, we'll make it work. I don't care as long as we're together." She was crying happy tears as she made her promise to always fight for them.

"Done. I don't ever want to be without you again. You're my first everything." He kissed her again, and it was deeper and hungrier.

Around them cheers and clinking glasses erupted.

"I wish Grandma Hattie could be here," she said under the festivities that were going on all around them.

"Oh, don't worry. She expects to see you tomorrow." Beau moved his mouth to her ear. "Now. Should we sneak you out to the bathroom? I saw you doing the pee dance."

ROCKIN' AROUND THE CHRISTMAS TREE

On Christmas Day, everyone in the Green household was partying at full force before the clock struck noon. The eggnog was already spiked, "Joy to the World" jingled and ricocheted off the walls, and about thirty pajama-clad people were staring in silent anticipation as Aubrey and Beau stood facing each other.

She squinted her eyes, halfway expecting the air to whistle and tumbleweeds to blow past them. He narrowed his eyes until they were barely slits, sending laser beams back at her, and Aubrey did her best not to laugh.

"Okay," Mom held her phone with her finger hovering over the green button. "Ready. Set. Go!"

Aubrey and Beau shook and bounced and twerked the tissue boxes strapped to their waists and the balls rumbled around within, most missed the opening.

"Shake!" Trey yelled.

The music changed, and suddenly Bing Crosby was singing "Silent Night," which threw their rhythm off.

As elegant and refined as she was in her red silk pajamas and fluffy on-theme buffalo check robe, Aubrey's mom lost her mind when it came to the minute-to-win-it games. She screamed for Aubrey to wiggle *then* bounce before she jumped up and down.

Sure enough, it worked. The orange ping-pong balls began to fall through the box opening, which sent Beau into overdrive.

"Come on, Grandma, I need a cheering section, too," he twerked hard, and his butt flipped up and down.

"You've never had that much rhythm," Grandma Hattie quipped, and everyone laughed. The uncoordinated shimmy, butt-rock he was doing did not make the balls come out. He resorted to gyrating and awkward hip winding.

Meanwhile, Aubrey was down to two balls.

"Go, Bree!" Matt and Sabrina called out together.

They were so cute. Since the engagement party, they'd been extra gooey with their PDA, which Aubrey surprisingly didn't mind. She and Beau had been doing plenty of the same.

One of Beau's balls finally popped out, setting him on fire. His butt kept shaking and the view wasn't bad, but it was too late. Aubrey's last ball hit the floor and her mom declared her the winner.

"Green gets it," she shouted triumphantly.

"Well, she won't be a Green much longer," Beau said, pulling Aubrey to him and kissing her. "Save some of that for tonight," he whispered.

Aubrey blushed and heat seared through her.

"All right, all right. Enough of that," her mom said. "Save it for the plane ride home. It's time for my famous Favorite Things gift exchange." She clearly loved the Christmas drill sergeant role and keeping everyone on schedule. Of course, she had a schedule and a checklist. The whole day planned out.

Beau released Aubrey. "Ellen, if you don't mind, I'd like to go first." Then he winked.

"What was that about?" Aubrey asked.

A vein at his temple twitched, and she knew whatever came

out of his mouth next would be a lie. "I…uh. Nothing, I just want to go first."

"Yeah, okay." Aubrey rolled her eyes and shrugged as he rounded the corner out of the living room into the kitchen.

When he returned, his hands were filled with an enormous box topped with an even larger bow. He placed it on the coffee table in front of Aubrey before sitting back on his heels to watch her expectantly.

"My favorite thing for my favorite person," he said.

Aubrey cut her eyes at him and slipped her bottom lip between her teeth. "Hmph. So you say. I hope you remember that when I'm up writing all night."

"Oh, I will. I'm just happy Gena offered you a remote staff writer position."

First, she shook the box. Then she beamed up at Beau. She was beyond happy, too. "No holes," she said, further inspecting the box. "Not a puppy or a chicken, unless you forgot and it's permanently sleeping."

A collective gasp sounded around the room.

"Kidding. I'm kidding. You guys are way too serious for Christmas Day—"

"Just open it already!" Matt yelled at her. "Good lord."

So she did. Or, at least she thought she did. She removed the bow and shook the box until the top slid off to reveal another box. "Seriously, Beau? You're doing this?"

"*We're* doing this." He nodded and seemed rather pleased with himself.

"Ugh."

Aubrey pulled the top of the second and third boxes off to reveal a fourth, fifth, sixth, seventh, and eighth box.

"Oh. My. God. I'm not opening another box," Bree said. "There had better be a million dollars in here or the key to a new Mercedes Benz." She fished through the boxes to the swishing sound of tissue paper. "If it's a sweater, I'm going to punch you in the throat."

"Aubrey Green. Try to be a lady," her mom chastised her.

Beau laughed. "Just keep going."

When she opened the fifteenth box, it contained a family-sized bag of Flamin' Hot Cheetos. She lurched across the table and toppled Beau to the floor. "You don't even like Cheetos!"

He kissed her and shielded his face with his arms. "I promise. It's a good thing. Just take them out of the box."

Slowly, she backed away, getting to her feet. "I'm on to you, Redgrave," she said, then gently tugged the bag from the box. Her heart flipped. Her eyes shot over to his and her face turned into a mess of emotions and blushed cheeks. She literally wanted to jump over the table again. Except, this time, she'd smother him with kisses and probably do something no one in the room should see.

"What it is?" Sabrina asked.

Aubrey jammed her hand into the box and held up a heart-shaped key ring with the word "home" engraved in the middle of it. Hanging from it was the single brass key to their place back in Vegas.

"This is *my* favorite thing!" She cried and met Beau's equally soggy gaze.

"Come back home with me," he said.

They both leaned over the table and met in the middle with a kiss.

The End

Thank you for spending your time with Bree and Beau. If you

enjoyed Wrapped Up in Beau, please consider leaving a *review* on **Goodreads** or your favorite online retailer.

Keep reading for an excerpt from
Mingle All the Way.
See what a serious (-ly fake) holiday office romance is like…

Join me in my reader group. I'd love to chat! That's where I connect with readers most.
Mia Heintzelman Reader Group

AN EXCERPT FROM — MINGLE ALL THE WAY

CHAPTER 1

"*H*ave ye no fear. She has arrived!" I sing, twirling over to my best friend, co-worker, and general event planning badass who's standing at a table at the back of the room. Nina is petite—barely up to my shoulder—and her thick, dark brown hair is in a perky ponytail. She's completely adorable. Also, I would do anything for her.

"Where do you need me? I brought a stopwatch—" I give the top button a click. It's responding ping is about as chipper as I am. "Just in case, I also brought my game face. This is Vegas. We can't be too careful."

Her perfectly micro-bladed brows dance as she gives me a quick once-over from my fabulous black thigh-high boots to my fierce red shift dress.

"*Yesss.*" She draws the word out, matching my dramatics with a snap of her fingers.

Nina darts her sparkly brown eyes over my shoulder as she tucks a glossy chestnut strand behind her ear. She leans in for a cheek-to-boob hug. Her cheek, my boob. *She's fun-sized.* I'm somewhere in between leggy volleyball player and WNBA player, though I am horizontally challenged. But, I digress.

I'm not here for men.

Just because I sell happily-ever-afters for the Lovestruck dating app doesn't mean it's a guaranteed employee benefit.

"She *is* ready. Red lips will do it every time," Nina continues.

"Bliss & Makeup Co. This is Crimson Queen," I say, filling her in on the best makeup to hit melanated girls since…ever. "Do yourself a favor and get one." I pucker, give her a shoulder shimmy and toss her a sweet smile.

She knows I'm not here to play around with these fools. This lipstick is all the drama allowed tonight.

"Girl, I've got this. Eight minutes sharp…like clockwork." I click the stopwatch button again for effect then whip my faux locs over my shoulder to the long line of bistro tables with flickering candles. Giant red Mylar heart balloons are strung with mistletoe over each two-seater table. "I'll usher the singles in. You'll do your little spiel, then the timed dates start. After, they'll have thirty minutes to mingle and fill out their little 'Let's make sparks' cards before I shuffle them out into the hands of the press for interviews."

I have a megawatt smile and arch a brow at her like, *they aren't even ready for all this, here.*

Nina's face twists with concern.

"What? You think they need more than half an hour to mingle?" I ask, failing to see the error in my plan.

It's the weekend after Thanksgiving. Technically, it's Small Business Saturday. No one is going to do anything to mess up the fat bonus coming my way when Nina pulls this event off. My plan is foolproof. Everyone who's anyone in Vegas is talking about it, and the PR companies are set to dutifully rave about it. When they do, ad sales on Cyber Monday will shoot through the roof, and Spencer James will be so thrilled, he'll gift everyone at Lovestruck financial tokens of his appreciation.

It's a no-brainer.

So, tonight there will be speed dating at this Lovestruck signature Mix'n'Mingle, but I will also duck and dive in and out of shadows to ensure things go off without a hitch.

When Nina doesn't verbalize what's screwing her face into a panic-stricken mess, my Spidey senses go off.

"Seriously, what?" I ask again. "Are you nervous? Did some guy already corner you? Because—"

"No. Nothing like that..." Nina's voice dies off, and I'm slightly relieved. These dating events can be dangerous for women in the game.

I don't know where men drew this conclusion, but for some reason, they think we're like some hyper-sexualized beings who love it when sleazy people aggressively "flirt" or demand reasons why we *shockingly*, don't want a second date.

Yeah, we love it when you make us feel unsafe in the name of love.

I have nothing against policing a bunch of people scheming for Christmas party plus-ones this time of year, but some people need to learn how to keep it classy.

That's what I'm here for.

"Actually..." Nina continues.

I busy myself tugging at the hem of my dress. I'm only halfway listening now because I've spotted the festive-looking open bar— my other excuse for showing up at a work event on my off day.

"Riley," Nina says my name flatly, which gets my attention.

"Yeah?"

"Change of plans. I need you in a *slightly* different capacity..." Her tense smile looks like it might snap at any second.

"Okaaay..." I drag the word out as I cock my head and narrow my gaze.

"Uh..." She scrunches her freckled nose and peeks an eye open. She's literally shaking in her open-toe booties. "The host from the speed-dating company has got all this stuff covered, so I don't actually need you to help *with* the speed dates. I need you to *be* a speed date."

See? I should've known this was too good to be true. My shoulders sag, and my head falls back as I groan. "What the heck, Nina? You know how I feel about dating in general. What makes you think I want to go on a dozen eight-minute dates all in one night? That's ninety-six excruciating minutes of hell for me. You do realize that, right?"

She sighs, and her big, pleading, puppy dog eyes land on me with full force. "It's the holidays," she whines. "You won't have to do the mingle part or the interviews. Two people canceled, and I don't have an even number for the rotations."

This time it's me who sighs—a massive, throaty, full chest heave. Then my thoughts snag on the first part of that sentence. *Two people.*

"Wait." My posture is ramrod straight now. I square my body to Nina and lean down to meet her eyes. "Who else did you get to fill in?"

No sooner is the question out of my mouth when I have my answer.

Chase Campbell from web development bounds through the double doors with a cocky half-grin and perfectly groomed beard. He looks like he ripped his fashion sense right out *GQ*'s Best-Dressed Men of the Week—the Irish edition. He's tall, muscly, and lean with carefree product-whipped red hair. He's also incredibly annoying because he knows he's gorgeous. *Ugh.* Of their own accord, my eyes take in his cuffed dark jeans and perfectly rumpled military-style green jacket, which I'm guessing is his version of no-fuss casual.

There's nothing subtle about the man wearing the prep-meets-free-spirit clothes, though.

Which is why I always ignore him.

Quickly, I avert my gaze and resort to fidgeting with my cuticles. I'm not part of the Chase Campbell fan club. I leave that to the girls in the marketing department.

Holidays or not, I'm not about to switch it up.

"All right. So, where do you need me? I ask.

Nina York flashes me a nervous smile. "Thank you so much for coming on such short notice, Chase. I'm totally going to owe you one." She shifts her body away from Riley Mills, whose tight red smile is fraying around the edges.

"Really. It's no problem. I'm happy to help," I say. I swear I hear a snort come from Riley, so reluctantly I tilt my head to meet Riley's steely gaze, careful not to gawk. "Hey, Riley."

She's tall with sculpted curves, long, shiny locs, and rich, dark skin. She's stunning in a way that always leaves me feeling blindsided, but she's also a serious suit in the most severe sense of the word—all day, every day. She doesn't even take off her jacket at the office despite the casual environment at the Lovestruck headquarters. At first, I thought it was because the A/C is always on high, but someone told me she lives by the "dress for the position you want" motto. Tonight, she must be throwing all that to the wind. The bare skin of her thighs that shows under the hem of her dress to the top of her boots…

The sight makes my stomach clench and sends a jolt right down to my dick.

Down, Chase. Barking up the wrong tree, here.

I swallow and avert my gaze because the reality is, I'm probably the last person Riley Mills expected to see tonight. I can tell the surprise isn't a welcome one.

The Lovestruck office is an open-air industrial building with strategically clumped cubicles meant to section off departments. She's in sales near event planning and marketing at the front of the building, and I'm in IT and web development way in the back by the emergency exit, which I've contemplated using on more than one occasion—anything to avoid passing her desk and the inevitable pursed-lip death stare she seems to reserve just for me.

Not that I have any clue why…

Even if it always looks like it kills her, we try to exchange minimal words—real gems like "hi," "hello," and "thanks for holding the door," which is usually growled. Other than those rare pleasantries, she seems to loathe me for reasons I'm still unaware. For her part, I suspect she interacts with me out of courtesy and professionalism, mostly. For me, it's a combination of fear and self-preservation, which is why I avoid her like the beautiful, bronze goddess plague that she is to my ego.

Nina clears her throat and flashes Riley a pointed stare. In an unexpected twist, Riley says, "Hi." It's like pulling teeth.

Now that wasn't so hard, was it?

Nina bounces up on her toes, breaking up the whole three-word conversation.

"So…" she rests her hands on my shoulders and lowers her chin before blurting out. "I need you to be one of the speed daters."

Oh, fuck. Why?

My gaze slides to Riley who crosses her arms over her chest and shakes her head. Right, she's been asked to be a date, too. So, somewhere in the rotation, Riley and I will be face to face for eight minutes.

In my book, that's plenty of time to get to the bottom of her apparent hatred for me.

Thanks, Nina.

"Yeah, I'm good. Whatever you need," I say with a shrug, doing my best to sound breezy and unaffected. On the inside, however, I'm rubbing my hands together at this twisted conspiracy Nina cooked up for us.

Or did she? Why would she?

Precisely ten minutes later, Nina and some young kid she has doing her gopher work let the singles in, and she gives her perky introduction speech, which is a bubbly welcome and thank you. Then she gives the rules of the event along with a warning about what would constitute dismissal from this event and all future events put on by Lovestruck. *Whoa, I guess she's not messing around.*

Half an hour later, I'm three dates in, two away from Riley, and I catch her sneaking glances over at me. I shoot her a confused look in return. That earns me a smile, which only makes my anticipation of our eight minutes together that much stronger.

Then, we're one table apart. She's with a typical tall, dark, and tattooed guy who is talking about his fitness training business, and I am with a raven-haired CEO who keeps going on about washi tape. *Whatever that is.* Much to my relief, Riley looks bored out of her mind.

When the timer goes off, and I switch into the chair in front of Riley, I go for it. "Want to tell me why you've been giving me the evil eye since date two?" I ask. *Oh, yeah, I'm going for it.*

She shakes her head and smiles. Maybe it's the candlelight flickering off her rich brown skin, or the way it glints off her eyes and turns them a warm shade of amber, but I'm mesmerized. I'm charmed by the prospect of graduating to two-word exchanges.

"Why are you even here? Isn't one of the marketing girls free tonight?" she asks with an eye roll.

Okay, a whole string of words. We're getting somewhere.

"Is that why you hate me?"

She presses a finger to her temple and massages like talking to me is *so* stressful. "Oh, your ego isn't massive or anything. Relax. Not everything is about you, believe me. I was just commenting on our work prospects. That's all." She presses the air with her palms.

There's something telling about the way she keeps looking away.

"Maybe, you don't hate me…because you like me." I cock my head to read her reaction.

"I don't date. Period."

So, you agree. You do like me.

I nod, and the corners of my mouth tug downward as my

lower lip protrudes. "Wow. So, what's this we're doing?" I lean in, forcing her gaze, and whisper, "It sort of feels like a date."

She parts her lips then closes them again.

"Just the facts." I shrug and lean back against my chair.

"I'm here as a favor to Nina just like you are, so save it. *And* there are free drinks. Don't go reading more into it." She runs a hand over the long black coiled strands of her hair. Then she surprises me. "I don't care how many minutes each date is, it's just nice to see a familiar face and have an unscripted conversation."

"So, you agree. It's nice to see my face…" I'm bobbing my head, biting back a shit-eating grin as a warm, musical laugh pipes out of her. I love this new unexpected banter between us. It's like we've been in the middle of a conversation all this time, and we've just jumped back in where we left off.

Then, the host, a tall, boisterous woman in a black jumpsuit with short platinum-blonde hair eases up to our table and positions the mic inches from her neon pink lips. "I want to pause for a few seconds. Go ahead. Stop the clock!" She gestures to Nina, who is all too happy to hear what the woman has to say.

The host flips the mic between Riley and me. "What are your names?"

We both hesitate, but eventually cave and tell her.

"Now, I don't mean to put you on the spot…" *Oh, sure you do.* "But I want everyone to stop what they're doing and take a look at Chase and Riley. They just met, what, four minutes and twenty-three seconds ago? Just like you. But I'll tell you a little secret. These two…they have it."

The room erupts into applause. Every pair of eyes in the place is on us. Honestly, I'm right there with this woman's assessment. She's not lying. The hair on my arms and the nape of my neck is raised. My heart is fluttering in my chest. I'm aching to reach across and touch Riley…or for her to touch me.

A slow smile tugs at the corners of my mouth until I see Riley's expression. She's tense. Her eyes dart to the host before landing—hard as bricks—on me.

"When the clock is ticking," the host continues, putting us directly on the spot despite the murder in Riley's eyes, "you can't get to know a person by asking their favorite color and what they do for a living. Questionnaires do not a connection make. You have to jump all the way in. These two are in each other's face, asking questions, smiling—I'm talking fierce eye contact, hair-touching, lips parted, leaning in. Yes, to all of it! The heat between these two is combustible."

In exactly this moment, I realize three fundamental truths. One, by the intensity of Riley's reaction, whatever this loathe-hate thing is, the feelings between us aren't one-sided. Two, the ache to touch her has spread to the growing hard-on in my pants. And three, the pursed-lip death stare is going to be epic on Monday.

Get **MINGLE ALL THE WAY** Now!

ACKNOWLEDGMENTS

No matter what you celebrate, I hope you enjoyed the spirit and cheer of the season in this one. The holidays are my favorite time of year because it reminds me that my time with my loved ones and friends is both precious and to be treasured. Wishing you and your families a safe, happy, and healthy holiday.

I have a ton of shout-outs to give because it took a lot of amazing people to help me get this fun story to market. Thank you to my Las Vegas Romance Writers family and especially my Thursday Night Therves. You are my fellow introverts uniting in dark corners and cozy nooks. You help me breathe life into my books and characters. Thanks for your invaluable, crazy, fun, and hashtaggable critique sessions.

To my editors at The Authors' Assistant, Danielle Acee and Danylle Salinas, I'm indebted to your polishing skills. You make my work shine. Thank you for your clear eyes and catching my "all" and "that" overuse.

A huge thank you to the librarians, bloggers, bookstagrammers, and reviewers. You are the unspoken heroes who spread the word like wildfire about stories, which feed the mind and nourish the soul.

Big hugs and smoochie kisses to my family and friends. You are the petals on my flowering tree and the frame holding up my house. You understand and support me even though I'm always with my nose stuck in a book or with my fingers glued to a keyboard spinning tales.

Mommy and Daddy I love that I'm equally both parts of your

(semi-) social butterfly (okay, sometimes, anti-) and bookworm because you've given me a hungry mind and wings to soar.

My sister, Melissa DeGrazia, we're basically the same person in two bodies fighting with our reflections, but who better to have in my corner to support and uplift me? Thank you. Cheers to leaping in faith!

Finally, to my two daughters and my nieces and nephews, I hope my daring pursuit of greatness is inspiration and wind beneath your wings.

ABOUT MIA HEINTZELMAN

Mia Heintzelman is a polka-dot-wearing, horror movie lover, who always has a book and a to-do list in her purse. When she isn't busy writing fictional happily-ever-afters, she is likely reading, or playing board games and eating sweets with her husband, two children, and fluffy goldendoodle pup. She writes fun, flirty, fiery romance about quirky, nerdy, strong women and the men with enough heart to fall for them.

Website:

miaheintzelman.com

Subscribe to My Newsletter:

miaheintzelman.com/newsletter.html

Join My FB Reader Group:

Facebook.com/groups/2219575585012649/

- instagram.com/miaheintzelmanauthor
- x.com/miaheintzelman
- facebook.com/miaheintzelmanauthor
- goodreads.com/miaheintzelman
- bookbub.com/authors/miaheintzelman
- amazon.com/author/miaheintzelman
- tiktok.com/@miaheintzelman

ALSO FROM MIA HEINTZELMAN

FORTEMANI FAMILY SERIES

LOVE, ROOTS, & WINE.

THE ACCIDENTAL CRUSH

LOVE & GAMES SERIES

ALL IS FAIR IN LOVE AND BOARD GAMES.

MONOPOLOVE

TRIVIALIZED PURSUIT

CLUED IN CHRISTMAS

TERMS & CONDITIONS SERIES

LOVE AND LAW. KNOW THE RULES, THEN BREAK THEM.

THE FRIENDSHIP CONTRACT

THE ALL MIXED UP SERIES

THEY CAN'T IGNORE THE LOVE SIGNS POINTING ALL AROUND THEM.

MIXED SIGNALS

MIXED MATCH

MIXED EMOTIONS

ALL MIXED UP - THE SERIES

STANDALONE ROMANCES

FAKE AROUND & FIND OUT

HOLIDAY ROMANCES

MISTLETOE. TWINKLE LIGHTS. ROMANTIC HOLIDAY NIGHTS.

MARRIED & BRIGHT

MINGLE ALL THE WAY

WRAPPED UP IN BEAU

COZY LITTLE CHRISTMAS

OLIVE & PEAR'S CHRISTMAS DETOUR

DARK ROMANCE

WASTELANDS ACADEMY SERIES

DEVASTATED

w/a EMMALINE ZANTHI

SEXY BWWM SHORT READS.

THE STACKS

THE BLUE GATE